Dragonology

DEMCO

Dragonology

CHRONICLES

⬦VOLUME THREE⬦

THE DRAGON'S APPRENTICE

Dugald A. Steer

illustrated by Nick Harris

CANDLEWICK PRESS

Text copyright © 2011 by Dugald A. Steer
Illustrations copyright © 2011 by Nick Harris

First U.S. edition 2011

Library of Congress Cataloging-in-Publication Data is available.

Library of Congress Catalog Card Number 2008938422

ISBN 978-0-7636-3427-8

11 12 13 14 15 16 BVG 10 9 8 7 6 5 4 3 2 1

Printed in Berryville, VA, U.S.A.

This book was typeset in Granjon.

Candlewick Press
99 Dover Street
Somerville, Massachusetts 02144

visit us at www.candlewick.com

For Max, Cameron, and Toby
D. S.

For my dear friend and guide, Virgil Pomfret
N. H.

PROLOGUE

On the morning of June 1, 1883, Major Cyril Wilson, a broad-shouldered, upright man, entered the Tower of London. Once inside, he made his way towards the ruins of the Lanthorn Tower, which was being excavated before it could be rebuilt. As he approached the scaffolding around the excavations, a figure stepped out of the shadows and walked towards him.

"Good morning, Major." The man raised his top hat in greeting.

"I take it that my equipment has arrived safely?" the major said.

The man nodded and led the major down some steps, then lifted a trapdoor to allow his visitor into an underground chamber.

"Knock when you're ready to come back up." The man handed the major a burning torch and left him to his business.

The chamber was roughly hewn and empty but for a long, leather case, which was propped against one wall, and a bundle of unlit torches. On the other wall, carved into the stone, was a massive shield, embossed with three lions. The major studied the shield for a moment and then pressed two fingers into the eyes of the topmost lion. There was a click, and the tongue of the second lion sprang out. The major gave it a sharp tug; with another click, the whole shield swung open to reveal a dark tunnel. As he held his torch aloft, the major's eyes widened. The flickering light revealed the tunnel to be stacked head-high on both sides with colossal bones. Fanged skulls jutted into the darkness, their shapes and outlines bearing little resemblance to the skulls of humans. These were the bones of monstrous beasts. Above the entrance were carved the words, *"Bienvenue au Royaume des Dragons Morts."*

" 'Welcome to the kingdom of dead dragons,' " the major murmured, translating the words to himself in a whisper. He drew out a map and studied it for a moment by the light of his torch. Then he picked up his case and strode purposefully into the bone-filled labyrinth.

An hour later, the major reached a lofty chamber. At the far end, a massive pair of double doors swung open on his approach. An unexpected waft of sulphur made him wrinkle his nose in disgust as he stepped into a huge, circular hall lit with blazing torches. Paintings and carvings of dragons decorated every surface, but the major's attention was drawn immediately to the opposite end of the hall, for there, rearing up on its hind legs—as though about to leap into the air—and towering above him, stood a life-size statue of a magnificent dragon, its wings outspread like a canopy just inches beneath the vaulted ceiling. The creature had giant rubies for eyes, scales of gold, and a protruding red tongue—a full three feet in length—that lolled from a mouth lined with vicious-looking silver teeth. But the statue was incomplete. Its right foreclaw was missing.

A sudden voice seemed to come from the very mouth of the statue: "Welcome! So you have come to join us?" The words echoed around the chamber.

"What is this place?" The major set down his case and gazed around in wonder.

"It is the grand lodge of the most Secret Order of Dragonsbane Knights," the voice replied. "Since the original knights are no longer with us, it now falls to others to continue with their quest."

"Their quest?" The major knew little about the task he had been summoned to perform.

"Look at the book."

By the foot of the dragon statue stood a lectern. It held an ancient book, covered with black leather and engraved in gold.

"*Malleus Draconis*' . . . ?" the major read aloud.

"*The Hammer of the Dragons*'! It was written by King Edward the First. To the knights, its word was law. Do you see the motto above the statue?"

The major studied the sculptured scroll above the head of the statue, and a shiver ran through him as he read the words, "*Mort aux Dragons.*"

"'Death to Dragons'! That was their battle cry!" The voice sounded eerie now. "Their mission was to kill every single dragon in the kingdom. They failed."

"So the bones in the labyrinth really are those of dragons?" The major had difficulty disguising the doubt in his voice.

"You are perceptive, Major."

"But dragons are creatures of myth."

"Of myth?" A man in a black frock coat stepped from behind the statue. His face was so hideously disfigured that its expression was impossible to read. "Behold!" He swept back an arm, dramatically gesturing towards a heavy iron portcullis that hung beneath a faded portrait of Saint George.

The major stepped closer. The sulphurous odour filled his nostrils now, and he clasped a hand to his mouth. Gazing drowsily up at him through the bars was a small green creature with furled wings. It stood upright and looked strangely human, though it was unmistakably a dragon. Its whiplike tail slapped the ground. The major lost a little of his usual composure and let out an audible gasp. "It is much smaller than I would have imagined." He studied the creature more closely and stiffened a little. "Can it really breathe fire?"

"Yes, but this variety does not often choose to do so. This is an infant gargouille dragon—hardly worth killing at all. But dragons grow bigger—much bigger. For an experienced soldier such as yourself, full-grown dragons are a great deal more satisfying to kill." The man gave a cruel, knowing smile. "When I sought you out, you told me the government was soon to take delivery of a powerful new artillery gun. For mountain warfare, you said. I believe you also claimed to be responsible for . . . testing it?"

"I have brought the weapon," affirmed the major, lowering his case to the floor.

"Then let us test it now." The man pulled a lever, and the portcullis retracted into the ceiling. The dragon stirred, slowly rose to its feet, and pulled feebly on the chain that attached it to the wall. The major undid the clasps on his case, lifted out a small field gun, and unfolded its legs. He placed the gun near the entrance to the hall and inserted a tapered shell into the muzzle.

"Stand behind me," the major ordered, more fiercely than he had intended. He cleared his throat and softened his voice a little. "This thing packs quite a punch."

The disfigured man did as he was told. The major knelt behind the gun and sighted along the barrel. The dragon blinked at him.

"It hardly seems sporting to kill a captive," the major protested, in the vain hope of appealing for a little compassion.

"Please proceed, Major." The man's eyes glinted, but the expression on his face remained impossible to read.

Finally, the major grimaced and pulled the trigger. Instantly there was a blinding explosion, resulting in a rising cloud of thick smoke. Silence followed. The smoke lifted. On the floor lay the motionless body of the dragon chick, its eyes staring, its acid blood fizzing out onto the flagstones.

The man approached it cautiously and prodded it with his toe.

"Is it dead?" the major asked.

"Yes." The man's face drew into a cold, lopsided smile, and he held out a gloved hand to the major.

"Now, Major. We have friends, but we also have enemies. Let me tell you about the Secret and Ancient Society of Dragonologists."

CHAPTER ONE
DRAGONSBROOK

We must discover all we can about those traitors
who assist dragons or enable them to remain
in hiding, and smite them without warning.
—— *Malleus Draconis (The Hammer of the Dragons), Edvardus Rex*

Torcher trotted happily along the forest path. He hopped over branches and trampled twigs underfoot. The brambles tore at his leathery skin, but his thick red scales were tough and he seemed untroubled by the thorns. Beatrice and I were less than impressed, however. "Will we always have to walk through the forest to get to Dragonsbrook?" I grumbled. It had been nearly an hour since we had left Castle Drake, and my pack was starting to weigh heavily on my shoulders.

"Only on dragonology-school days," Mother answered cheerily.

"Isn't there an easier way to get there, though?" asked Beatrice, a little breathless as she clambered up a steep, muddy bank.

"This is the quickest route from Castle Drake." Already at the top of the bank, Father turned and pointed across a dense cluster of trees behind him. "But you can also reach it along a track on the other side of the forest."

"Wouldn't it be wonderful if we could ride here on ponies?" Beatrice suggested, suddenly hopeful. "Then we could go round the long way, but it would take far less time."

Mother laughed affectionately and offered her free hand to pull Beatrice up to the top of the bank. "You want to ride a nice, fat little pony when there are hungry dragons around?"

"The ponies don't have to be fat. . . ." Beatrice pleaded.

Mother shook her head gently. "I'm sorry, Beatrice, but dragons and ponies do not mix."

"If Torcher were big enough, he could fly us there," I ventured. Everyone laughed, and Torcher puffed out a tiny flame, perhaps pleased that we were talking about him.

Torcher was our European dragon chick, and he was still only one year old. Beatrice and I had hatched him from his egg. We'd been raising him ever since and had grown very fond of him.

"Of course," Mother reminded us, darkening the mood again, "once Torcher is big enough for you to ride him, he'll be ready to return to the wild." We could hardly bear the thought that we would one day be parted from our favourite dragon. Father knew as much, and he quickly changed the subject.

"Torcher will love Dragonsbrook," he suggested, striding

off sideways along the path so that he could stay ahead but still talk to us. "He'll have much more freedom. And in any case, if we're going to run a refuge for orphan dragon chicks, it has to be remote. We can't risk just anyone finding out about it."

"Isn't Castle Drake remote enough already?" Beatrice quickened her pace to catch up with him. "Anyway, what will happen when it rains?"

"You can take an umbrella!" Father raised his eyebrows and pretended to rebuke her. "Can this be the girl who has flown halfway around the world on the Dragon Express, camped out under the stars, and endured the blistering heat of the Sahara and the icy cold of the Himalayas?"

"Well," she mused, linking arms with Father, "it wasn't raining then."

My sister and I were both really excited about the dragon refuge, but most of all, we were delighted that we would be living together with our parents again. We had spent a full four years apart from them, whilst Father and Mother were out in India carrying out important investigations for the Secret and Ancient Society of Dragonologists. They had been surprised and delighted when Beatrice and I had found them in the Himalayas on our mission to save the naga dragons. The experience had very nearly ended in disaster, however, and now our parents had decided that we should spend some time together as a proper family.

We also loved the dragonology school, especially now that we had new friends there. Billy Light was an old hand at Dr. Drake's school, having started a year ahead of us, but Alicia, his younger sister, had joined at the same time as us. They were the children of Lewis Light, better known to us as Lord Chiddingfold, the government's secret Minister for Dragons. Billy was friendly, but a bit of a know-it-all, and he was always putting his sister down. However, since she'd met Beatrice, Alicia was beginning to fight back, and Billy even seemed to appreciate it.

Darcy Kemp had started at the school before us as well, and he was lucky enough to help out at Dr. Drake's Dragonalia — Dr. Drake's London shop — from time to time. He was slightly older than us, and, when it came to dragons, he certainly knew what he was talking about.

Suddenly, under a clump of bracken leaves at the foot of a birch tree, I spotted a patch of purple gloop oozing onto the path and recognized it at once as knucker venom. It was a clear sign that Weasel, the local knucker dragon, was about. I called the others to take a look.

Beatrice was alarmed. "Where's Torcher?"

"Up ahead somewhere, I think," I told her.

The last time they had met, Torcher, who was only a tenth of Weasel's size at the time, had given the poor knucker such a fright that she had hidden in her hole for two whole weeks. We glanced around, but Torcher was nowhere to be seen.

Striding ahead once again, Father stopped in a broad clearing and turned back to wait for us. As we approached, we could see shafts of sunlight warming the crumbling remains of a wall. The stone building next to it was so completely covered in brambles and ivy that it was impossible to pick out any features.

"Look at the state of this old ruin!" Beatrice scoffed, and at once, Mother guffawed with laughter. "What's so amusing?" asked Beatrice, perplexed.

Mother did not have time to answer, however, as Torcher, who had actually fallen behind us, suddenly raced past, hugging his leathery wings in to his sides and wriggling his scaly body through the broken bars of the ruin's rusty gate. A thin column of smoke was rising up from what must have been a chimney at the top of the building.

"Ah, Mademoiselle Gamay must have arrived," said Mother. She unlatched the gate and followed Torcher down the overgrown path.

Beatrice's jaw dropped in horror. "You don't mean that this is where we're going to be living? *This* is Dragonsbrook?"

"Don't let first impressions fool you," said Father, studying the walls carefully. "Once we get that ivy off, you'll soon see how pretty it is." As if determined to prove his point, he pulled a small machete from his backpack and began hacking away at the bushes by the gate.

"Where are the orphan dragons going to stay?" wailed Beatrice. "And what about Torcher?"

"Well, the orphaned dragons can be housed in the old stable block around the back," Father answered, "and Torcher has a choice of two possible lairs. We'll show you those later.

But first we want you to inspect the cottage; we thought you children would be eager to choose your rooms."

"So Torcher won't be staying in the house, then?" I asked, disappointed.

"You know perfectly well, Daniel, that we can't have dragons living in the house with us," Father answered sternly. "It's far too dangerous."

"Has anyone told Torcher that?" I could see his scaly tail disappearing under the curtain of ivy that hung over the front door.

"Well, don't just stand there." With an exasperated look on his face, Father clapped his hands loudly as if to shoo us away. "Go after him!"

Beatrice and I hurried after Torcher into the dim interior of the cottage.

"So this is our new home," I said. Even in the darkness, I could pick out the cracks and cobwebs on the ceiling — there were so many of them!

"How can you call it a home?" Beatrice protested. "It's dark and spooky, and I hate it."

We advanced through the gloom, feeling our way along the hall towards the back of the house, our eyes slowly adjusting to the darkness.

"Torcher?" I called. There came a sudden clatter of falling pots and pans, followed by a high-pitched scream. Beatrice jumped, and I heard a voice exclaim, *"Sacré bleu! What is going on?"*

It was Mademoiselle Gamay, Dr. Drake's housekeeper. She also taught certain dragonology lessons; she was a highly respected French dragonologist. Today, however, she'd come to help us prepare the cottage.

Beatrice and I stared in astonishment as an upturned black cooking pot floated around the side of the door at the end of the hall, a full three feet above the ground.

"I knew it!" cried Beatrice. "This house is haunted!"

My sister glared at me as I began to laugh. "It's not haunted," I exclaimed. "It's just Torcher!"

Even Beatrice smiled at that. "Hmm, very stylish, Torcher." She giggled.

Inside the pot, Torcher was making a *poh, poh, poh* sound. Beatrice and I looked at each other, and our smiles broadened.

"Is he trying to say 'pot'?"

"I think so," cried Beatrice. Delighted, she rushed across to reward Torcher with a hug. "Clever dragon. Yes, you have got your head stuck in a *pot,* and Mademoiselle Gamay would like it back now, thank you very much."

"I suppose we had better de-pot him before he does any damage," I said.

Beatrice nodded and took hold of Torcher's wriggling back legs whilst I grabbed the pot end.

"On the count of three, pull!" cried Beatrice.

"One, two —" I began.

"*Hic!*" Torcher hiccupped.

"Uh-oh!" said Beatrice, a look of panic on her face. "We had better move quickly."

We bundled the little dragon out the front door, dropped him, and quickly leapt away. Torcher only ever hiccupped when he was about to breath fire, and sure enough, seconds later, a long sheet of flame burst from beneath the edges of the pot, scorching off a large section of the ivy that hung over the front door. Still in the dark, the dragon chick stumbled around until, at last, he crashed into the garden wall. He bashed his head against the brick once, twice, then a third time, and the pot finally fell to the ground with a clang.

"And they say Torcher is one of the intelligent dragons!" Mademoiselle Gamay scoffed. She had followed us outside and now stood over him with her hands on her hips. "*Mon dieu!* Save us from the stupid ones!"

Grabbing the dragon chick by the nape of his neck, she wiped his sooty face with a corner of her apron. "There," she said. "That is a bit more presentable." She let him go and turned to Beatrice and me. "And what's wrong with Torcher's keepers today? Perhaps we should discuss the importance of attentiveness in our next dragonology class?"

"We're sorry," Beatrice answered, carefully studying the overgrown lawn at her feet.

"We should have kept a closer eye on him," I added sheepishly.

"Never mind about Torcher now, children." Mother approached and flung an arm around each of us. "I'll keep an eye on him whilst you two go and choose your rooms."

"Race you!" Beatrice cried, but she was already charging back inside and was soon halfway up the stairs, which ran through the middle of the cottage. I chased after her, but she stuck out her elbows and stopped me from getting past.

Immediately at the top of the stairs, on either side, were two doorways. Beatrice disappeared into one, so I decided to investigate the other.

The room had a large bay window and a door that led on to another, smaller room lined with narrow shelves. It was the perfect space for a dragonological laboratory.

"I bag this room," I called to Beatrice.

"But you haven't seen this one yet," Beatrice called back.

"Well, I'm happy here." Surely the other room couldn't be any better.

"I'll have this one, then," Beatrice answered. "And no changing your mind once you've seen mine." She sounded rather too pleased with herself, and I began to wonder whether I had made the right choice.

At last, curiosity got the better of me, and I decided to go see for myself. Beatrice's room was a lot smaller than mine, but on the far side a narrow, wrought-iron stairway twisted up to a square turret room in the roof of the cottage. I hadn't noticed it from the outside because of all the ivy. I looked around. Why, oh, why did I always have to be so hasty?

"This is exactly the sort of room a dragonologist ought to have," I said. "But it's far too good for a girl, you know."

"What utter rot!" retorted Beatrice indignantly. "It's perfect for Q.T.B."

Beatrice had her own club, rather annoyingly called Quicker Than Boys. Obviously I wasn't allowed to be a member, and why would I want to join a ridiculous girls' club, anyway? We were quiet for a moment. I supposed there would be no chance of wrangling the room from Beatrice's clutches now, but it was worth a try.

"So you've changed your mind about Dragonsbrook?" I asked.

"It might not be as bad as I first thought," Beatrice admitted.

"Let's toss a coin to see who gets which room," I suggested.

Beatrice wagged her finger at me. "Not a chance. We agreed no going back, remember? I might let you come up here sometimes, if you are nice to me and when there is no Q.T.B. meeting, of course. We can do our dragonology homework here together."

I peered out through a dusty window to the garden far below. Mother was standing with Torcher next to a large pile of garden debris. She was tickling the little dragon's chin to make him breathe fire and start a bonfire. Meanwhile, Father was still hacking away at some overgrown bushes with his machete. I glanced back along the path we had taken to reach the house, and noticed a movement.

"Look!" I said. "Someone is coming towards the house."

Beatrice joined me at the window. "It's Dr. Drake, isn't it? I thought he was away for another week."

"He looks really tired," I observed. "Do you think he's all right?"

Down in the garden, Mother had seen Dr. Drake, too. She rushed to greet him. A moment later, Father and Mademoiselle Gamay joined them. They looked very concerned. Dr. Drake was relating something in earnest, and I saw Mother glance up in our direction.

"Let's go down and see him," said Beatrice. "It certainly looks as though something has happened."

After our triumph at the Battle of Hong Wei, in China, it was presumed that the Russian Alexandra Gorynytchka, who had been responsible for the poisoning of the naga dragons, had died. However, soon afterwards, rumours had spread that she had survived her cliff-top plunge and now had a new scheme to enslave all dragons. Dr. Drake had left to investigate the rumours some weeks earlier.

When we reached the garden, the adults looked up at us and stopped talking immediately. Dr. Drake rose wearily to his feet and held out his arms.

"How are my favourite young dragonologists?" he asked, smiling. "And what is your opinion of Dragonsbrook? I think this will be an excellent spot for a dragon orphanage, don't you agree?"

Dr. Drake took off his cap and wiped his forehead, then sat back down heavily.

"Is there something wrong, Dr. Drake?" asked Beatrice.

The doctor waved his hand dismissively. "Nothing for you two to worry about. I am tired; that is all. I have been very busy." He smiled again and said brightly, "Your mother says that you have been busy choosing your rooms. Have you each found one you like?"

We both nodded enthusiastically.

"Good. So perhaps now it is time Torcher chose his new lair. There is a bank on the other side of the stable block, where you will find two small caves. Why don't you take him down there and see which one he likes best?"

We soon found the caves. It seemed they had once been used as storerooms. One of them had a wooden door, whilst the other had a rusty metal grille. Torcher explored each in turn.

"Well, that got rid of us." I gave Beatrice a knowing look.

"Why does Dr. Drake look so worried?" she asked anxiously. "Whatever it is, he obviously doesn't want us to know about it. Although, to my mind, knowing nothing is much worse than knowing the truth. It will only make us worry more."

"Let's go and listen to what the grown-ups are saying." I started moving slowly back towards the cottage. "If it's really serious, we need to know."

Beatrice looked shocked at my suggestion, and I stopped in my tracks, but then she nodded and gave a wry smile. "For once, Daniel, I agree with you."

"What about Torcher?" We watched him waddle out of the second cave, back into the first, then out of the first and back into the second.

"Torcher's all right. He's making up his mind. Come on."

We crept back up the bank as quietly as we could until we reached the end of the stable block, where we could eavesdrop easily on the adults.

"Did Idraigir say *how* Brythonnia was attacked?" Mother was asking, her face creased with worry.

"There was an explosion," replied Dr. Drake. "Two of the side tunnels leading to her lair were completely destroyed. Fortunately, Brythonnia was unharmed. From the smell, Idraigir believes the explosion was caused by dynamite."

"Dynamite?" Father was astonished. "Do you think the culprit knew he was trying to blow up a dragon's lair?"

"Most probably," said Dr. Drake, removing his hat and running a hand through his grey hair. "Of course, whoever it was *might* have stumbled across the tunnels by accident, but it seems unlikely. Brythonnia is extremely wary of humans and almost impossible to surprise. And then there is the matter of the signet ring that was found on the mountain slope outside her lair. A ring that was engraved with a very distinctive *D*-rune."

"You don't mean — ?" Mother gasped in alarm.

"Yes." Dr. Drake nodded his head gravely. "I'm afraid I do."

"But I thought that the murderous knights who wore those rings were defeated centuries ago?" Father spoke through gritted teeth.

"So did we all," agreed Dr. Drake.

"Was there any other evidence of Brythonnia's attacker?" asked Mother.

"Well, I'm afraid that the perpetrator was rather hoist with his own petard: he was blown up with his own dynamite. A fitting end, perhaps, but his body was destroyed, leaving us with no clues as to who might have been responsible."

Mother raised a hand her mouth. "Whatever shall we tell the children?"

"Tell them nothing for the time being," said Dr. Drake kindly. "I don't think we should worry them, though they will have to hear about the attack sooner or later. I am still hoping they will attend the ceremony, by the way. The Dragon Rite has been moved up. Idraigir is adamant that the Society of Dragons should be as strong as possible to meet this new threat — whatever, or whoever, is behind it."

Beatrice turned to me anxiously. "What on earth is so special about a ring with a *D*-rune?" she whispered.

"I don't know," I replied. "But if the dragons are under threat, we will need to take extra-special care of Torcher."

✦ ✦ ✦

We would not be able to move in to Dragonsbrook for a while yet, and so we returned to Castle Drake that evening to discover that Dr. Drake had departed for a meeting with Lord Chiddingfold in London. He had left instructions that, even though Beatrice and I were to spend our mornings helping our parents prepare Dragonsbrook, classes in dragonology would continue at Castle Drake in the afternoons under the guidance of Mademoiselle Gamay.

Darcy was the only other student at the school at that time, and before our lesson started the following afternoon, we quickly recounted everything we had overheard. We knew he would be able to give us some answers.

Darcy's brow furrowed. "Brythonnia is a very powerful European dragon from Cumbria. She has a terrible distrust of humans — and no wonder, by the sounds of it." We pressed him for more information.

"Apparently, a signet ring bearing a *D*-rune was discovered on the mountain outside Brythonnia's lair," I said. "Mother and Father both seemed really alarmed when Dr. Drake mentioned it."

Darcy's frown deepened. He clenched his fists. "So the rumours are true?"

"What rumours?" I asked.

"That the dragon slayers have returned! I overheard Dr. Drake say something about it to Lord Chiddingfold."

"Then what does the ring mean?" Beatrice persisted.

"It is almost certainly a Dragonsbane ring," said Darcy. "I'm not surprised you haven't heard the name; members of the S.A.S.D. don't usually say the word out loud. It's a matter of respect for the dragons that were slain. But you have studied S.A.S.D. history. If you remember, the Order of Dragonsbane Knights was a secret order formed by King Edward Longshanks. The knights had a single aim: to slay every dragon in the kingdom. Their methods were foul, and they grew rich from the hoards they pillaged from the dragons. They would quite likely have succeeded in wiping out all dragons in this country had not Beatrice Croke and her son, Daniel, stopped them by forming the S.A.S.D. and allying themselves with the newly formed Society of Dragons."

"But surely that is ancient history," I scoffed. "How on earth could an order of medieval knights still be active today?"

"I don't know. But if they are, it will be a terrible day for dragons — indeed, for all of us."

We were silent for a moment, and I struggled to understand what Darcy was suggesting. A sudden, chilling thought occurred to me: "Do you think Alexandra Gorynytchka could be behind it all?" I asked.

To my surprise, Darcy shook his head vigorously. "No. Even Alexandra doesn't want to destroy dragons. Her aim is to make them her slaves in order to use their power."

"You're right." Beatrice nodded thoughtfully. "And anyway, I can't see her using dynamite to kill dragons when she still has a weapon like the Spear of Saint George in her possession."

"What about Ignatius?" I asked.

Darcy looked surprised. "So you haven't heard the news? According to Dr. Drake, Ignatius Crook is dead."

I was astonished. Ignatius was the son of one-time Dragon Master Ebenezer Crook. Sadly, he had not inherited his father's concern and sympathy for dragons. Instead, his greed and lust for power had led to the death of the Guardian Dragon two years earlier. The last we had heard of him, he was in Paris, searching for Alexandra Gorynytchka.

"Is he really dead?" I asked, still finding the news hard to take in. "How did he die?"

"I don't know. But we're bound to learn more at the Dragon Rite."

"We keep hearing about this Dragon Rite," said Beatrice. "But I've no idea what it is. That's yet another thing we've been kept in the dark about."

Darcy's eyes sparkled as he pictured the event. "Ah," he answered wistfully, "it is the ceremony to invest a new Guardian Dragon. It has only ever happened once before, when the Society of Dragons was founded. All the members of the S.A.S.D. and the Society of Dragons are invited. It will be such a spectacle!"

At last, the cottage was ready for us. Beatrice and I settled quickly into our rooms, and Torcher made it clear that he had decided to make his new lair in the cave with the wooden door. It would be some time before we would be able to take in any orphaned dragons, and so our next task was to help flameproof the stable block in preparation for their arrival.

Dr. Drake had not returned from London, but judging by the number of whispered conversations that stopped abruptly as soon as Beatrice or I arrived, it was obvious that a lot more was going on than the failed attack on Brythonnia. Of course, as we weren't supposed to know anything, we couldn't very well ask for details, and we hadn't heard another word about the Dragon Rite, so we were astonished when we returned home from Castle Drake one evening to find Torcher waiting for us with a piece of shed dragon skin in his mouth.

"Where did you get that from?" I bent to examine it. Torcher clamped his prize tightly between his sharp teeth. "It's not yours, is it?"

"Are you colour-blind, Daniel?" Beatrice scolded. "Torcher's scales are red, not green." She peered at the skin closely, then gasped. "It's covered in runic writing. It must be a message from the Society of Dragons!"

We had received such a message only once before, but I clearly remembered how the runes had started to fade as soon as they were exposed to the light. "We'd better read it quickly, before the writing disappears," I urged.

Beatrice went to tug the message gently from Torcher's jaws. He wouldn't let go at first, but when she stroked his forehead gently, he closed his eyes, pulled back his head, and released the skin into her hand. Beatrice unfolded it carefully and read aloud:

"To the Cook Family
From the Council of Seven Dragons

You are cordially invited to attend a Dragon Rite to witness the grand investiture of the new Guardian Dragon. We shall also require the presence of the one known as Torcher, son of Scramasax. Please be sure to bring him with you. Be ready for transportation to Wharncliffe at three o'clock tomorrow afternoon. Until then, go with dragon speed!

The Society of Dragons."

Tomorrow seemed an eternity away; we could hardly contain our excitement.

CHAPTER TWO

THE DRAGON RITE

Seek out the dragons' most secret places, yea, even
in the very depths of the earth, where they guard
their hoards and hatch their scaly broods.

—— *Malleus Draconis (The Hammer of the Dragons), Edvardus Rex*

The next afternoon, just before three o'clock, Beatrice and I stood in front of the window of the tower room, eagerly scanning the sky.

"There!" I cried, pointing to a dot in the distance. "Is that a dragon, do you think? Next to that cloud—the one that's shaped like a man's head?"

Beatrice was shading her eyes with her hand. "That looks more like a bird to me," she said. "Are you sure you don't need spectacles, Daniel?"

"Very amusing." I sniffed. "But maybe we should keep a pair of binoculars up here."

Suddenly, two huge European dragons—one green and the other gold—swooped down over the trees on the far side of the glade, casting a vast shadow across the garden.

"It's Idraigir." Beatrice gasped. "And another dragon I don't recognise. I wish I knew how they managed to get so close without us seeing them."

The dragons circled the glade, checking that it was safe to land. Idraigir set himself down expertly in front of the cottage, whilst the golden dragon, who was only a shade smaller than Idraigir, touched down in the yard in front of the stable block. Each wore an intricately carved dragon saddle, quite different from the leather and wooden models I had seen before. These saddles had high pommels inlaid with precious stones and girths that fastened with wide gold buckles. They looked as though they had been made centuries ago.

"We're not the only ones wearing our Sunday best!" Beatrice said with a laugh as we raced down the stairs two at a time.

We reached the garden just as Mother and Father arrived. Idraigir was already touching noses with Torcher.

"Praisich hoyari!" Idraigir exclaimed in Dragonish. "Allow me to make an introduction." He inclined his head towards his companion. "I am proud to present Brythonnia."

I was astonished. So this was Brythonnia. She was indeed a magnificent dragon. I wondered how anyone could have considered destroying such a creature.

"Brythonnia dwells in the place you call Cumbria," continued Idraigir. "Normally she will only speak Dragonish or Latin, but as we meet today for such a special occasion, she is prepared to make an exception."

"Praisich boyar," Beatrice greeted the dragons politely.

"Ave!" I said, proud that I still remembered a few words of Latin from my boarding-school days.

"Praisich boyar! You are most welcome," said Father. "It has been many years since we last met."

Brythonnia dipped her golden head slightly and replied, *"Praisich!"* Her voice sounded slightly hoarse, perhaps from lack of use, I thought. "Years pass quickly for me," she told us. "Being one who prefers to avoid the society of others, I mostly keep my own company and my own counsel."

As the golden dragon extended her long neck towards Beatrice and me, her large, bright eyes betrayed no emotion. Her hot, sulphurous breath stung my face as she sniffed us, and it was a considerable relief when she pulled back her head again.

"So these human chicks are Dr. Drake's most recent pupils?" There was a note of uncertainty in her voice as she addressed Idraigir. "We are grateful to them for saving us from the plague, are we not? I hope that they give us no cause for disappointment in the future."

"They are still children," Idraigir replied kindly. "If they do not always please you, then try to judge them mercifully."

"Greetings, children," Brythonnia said, turning to us. "The fame of your brave deeds has preceded you. Idraigir trusts you, and so we are joined as allies."

"Brythonnia and I have come here to take you to the Dragon Rite." Idraigir was starting to look a little agitated.

"Now that you have been introduced, we must not delay further."

So Father lifted Beatrice and Torcher onto the soft leather saddle on Idraigir's back. Then he pushed me on in front of them, and I grasped the pommel. Beatrice held on to my waist, and with Torcher resting across her lap, we were ready to fly.

"Are you comfortable?" asked Father, smiling proudly at the sight of us.

"They should be." Idraigir seemed to smile in return. "These double saddles are very special. They were made long ago solely for occasions such as this."

Brythonnia crouched down, allowing Mother and Father to clamber up onto her saddle.

"It will be just like old times!" cried Idraigir, stretching up to his full height. He gave a roar that echoed around the forest, then bounded across the glade and took off effortlessly, rising on swift wings through a dense patch of cloud, until the forest and Dragonsbrook seemed little more than minute toys beneath us.

Some three hours later, we crossed the moor and descended towards Wharncliffe. The dragons landed with ease, and we thanked them as we dismounted.

"It is as Idraigir requested," Brythonnia answered graciously. "Go with dragon speed."

Idraigir stretched a wing gently around our dragon chick and began leading him away. "Torcher will come with us," the great dragon told us. "There are things he must learn before the ceremony begins. You four must wait with the other members of the Secret and Ancient Society." Idraigir pointed a claw towards a figure outlined in the mist on the barren moor. He wore a large, flowing cloak with the hood pulled so far across his face that we could see none of his features. As we approached, the figure stood tall, and I jumped as he suddenly swung down a long, heavy dragon-headed staff to bar our way.

"Stay!" he cried. "I am the door warden of the Guardian's Chamber. Before I can let you pass, I must confirm that you are members of the Secret and Ancient Society of Dragonologists."

His voice was so stern and his appearance so sinister and commanding that I almost forgot I really was a member of the society.

"When a dragon flies . . . ?" he demanded. There was something strangely familiar about his voice, but I couldn't place it.

"He seeks it with his eyes," I replied as boldly as I could.

"And when he slumbers deep . . . ?"

"He dreams of it in sleep," Beatrice answered this time. I heard her voice falter a little and could tell she was feeling the same as I was.

"And what is the answer to the riddle?" the man continued solemnly.

"Treasure!" Beatrice and I almost squeaked together.

"All four of you are members of the Secret and Ancient
Society?"

Mother and Father spoke with us this time: "We are."

"Then you may pass with the Sign of the Dragonological
Apprentice."

As we had been taught, all four of us held our right
hands in loose fists with one finger pointing towards the
ground. The hooded figure stepped back, and with relief,
we entered the tunnel that led to the Guardian's Chamber.
The hooded man followed us inside and pulled the stone
door shut behind him. Then he led us deeper and deeper
into the tunnel.

"Are we sure it's safe?" I whispered, searching anxiously
for signs of cracks in the torch-lit ceiling. Beatrice and I had
been through this tunnel once before with Dr. Drake. "It
was full of falling boulders the last time we were here."

"Of course it's safe," Beatrice chided. "The dragons have
cleared away the rocks. They wouldn't bring us all here if
they thought it was dangerous, now, would they?"

Our parents, however, had not had occasion to visit the
Guardian's lair before. We reached the chamber at last,
and Beatrice and I smiled at each other as we watched our
mother and father suddenly stop dead, then gasp in awe.
They were standing at the edge of a deep chasm. From a

tall platform in the chasm's very centre, the Guardian's vast treasure hoard glittered and sparkled.

At last the cloaked figure pulled back his hood, and I almost laughed to see that it was none other than Mr. Flyte, from Dr. Drake's Dragonalia, who had followed us into the chamber. Though he sometimes disagreed with Dr. Drake on matters dragonological, he was hardly a sinister character.

"It looks as though we are the last to arrive," Father observed. A short distance away, Dr. Drake and a number of others were clustered on our side of the cavern. Emery, Mademoiselle Gamay, and her brother, Bernard, stood to the left of Dr. Drake, whilst Billy, Alicia, and Darcy stood to his right. Farther along, the Minister for Dragons, Lord Chiddingfold, and his bad-tempered private Secretary, Mr. Tibbs, were exchanging quiet words with a tall, imposing-looking man. I recognised him immediately from his distinctive white hair and bushy sideburns. It was none other than Mr. Gladstone, our Prime Minister! This was indeed a special occasion.

"Are we supposed to do anything?" I whispered to Mother.

"No!" she replied, raising a finger to her lips. "But shhh! They are about to start."

A few moments later, our whispers were hushed by the resounding clang of a bell. A deep and reverent silence filled the cavern. Then, all at once, a roar boomed up from the depths of the chasm that seemed louder than thunder. It grew gradually stronger until I could feel it throbbing in my very bones. Six dragons had joined their voices in a wild chorus. Suddenly, a brilliant blaze of dragon fire lit up the cavern as those dragons appeared on the opposite side of the chamber.

I knew the first two—Idraigir and Brythonnia—but the others I had not seen before. Three of them were adults, but the last was a good deal smaller, perhaps twenty feet long and a mere thirty years old. In dragon terms this was an adolescent, and unlike the European dragons, he was coloured pure white. Given that frost dragons were not native to Britain, I had not expected one to belong to the Society of Dragons. I nudged Beatrice and attempted to point whilst no one was looking. But then my attention was drawn elsewhere, for silhouetted against the glow of dragon fire stood a man, dwarfed by his scaly companions, his arms raised high above his head. As my eyes adjusted to the brightness, I saw that it was none other than Dr. Drake, holding aloft the Dragon's Eye—the ancient gem that symbolized his status as Dragon Master. The six dragons roared again as one.

"Who comes to bear witness to this Council of Seven Dragons?" Idraigir demanded fiercely.

"I do!" exclaimed Dr. Drake, his voice grave with the solemnity of the occasion. "The old Guardian lies slain. Yet an ancient danger grows. A new Guardian must be chosen from among you. I have come to bear witness."

"By what right do you desire to witness the deeds of dragons?"

"By my right as Dragon Master, bestowed upon me by the Guardian that was slain," replied Dr. Drake.

"By which word did you become Dragon Master?" Idraigir was similarly solemn, his voice slow and clear.

"DRACO-RACO-ACODRAC!"

"Is this word safe?" the dragon demanded.

"It has become known by our enemies. A replacement is needed." There were quiet murmurs among the spectators.

"One shall be offered," said Idraigir graciously. "Do you know the form of words used in the ceremony?"

"I do."

"Then step forward and speak them, Dragon Master!"

Idraigir's tail snaked out and curled around Dr. Drake's waist, then lifted him over the chasm and placed him on the central platform, where he stood atop a huge pile of treasure.

"Who attends the Council of the Seven Dragons?" It now fell to Dr. Drake to question the dragons, first in English and then in Dragonish. Each dragon responded in both languages, their voices echoing around the cavern and sending shivers tingling down my spine.

"Idraigir of Cader Idris."

"Brythonnia of Helvellyn."

"Somerled of Cape Wrath."

"Tregeagle of the Lizard."

"Ambrosius of Avebury."

"Erasmus of Anglia."

"And what of the last?" Dr. Drake called out. "Where is the seventh dragon?"

"The seventh dragon is Scramasax of Ben Wyvis, known as the Dornoch Wyrm," answered Idraigir.

"She is not here?" Dr. Drake did not seem surprised.

"She cannot be with us. She has suffered a grievous wound, which even yet has not fully healed."

"Who gave her that wound?"

"I did," Idraigir answered calmly. Murmurings began among the spectators once again. "Though it was against my will."

"Who shall answer for her?"

"Her son is here. He shall stand in her stead." Did they mean Torcher? I could hardly believe what I was hearing. So our little dragon really was going to take part in the Dragon Rite.

"Then let him step forward!"

I turned to Beatrice. She seemed just as surprised as I was.

Torcher trotted out from behind the other dragons. He acted quite untroubled, despite being dwarfed by his companions. Beatrice and I exchanged proud glances.

"What is your name, dragon?" Idraigir asked.

"Torcher!" our little chick answered with a confident roar.

I gasped and turned again to Beatrice. "He's never said his name before. Maybe that is what Idraigir wanted to teach him?"

"Shh!" Mother gave me a stern look.

"Welcome, Torcher of Dragonsbrook," Idraigir continued. "In the name of the Guardian and of dragons slain and of the ancient pact between men and dragons since the time of Dragonsbane, do you swear to join this council, to offer opinion when it is requested, and to abide by its lawful judgements in your mother's stead until she is healed?"

"*Ssssorrr!*" Torcher answered boldly, using the Dragonish word for yes.

"Will you swear to assist the bearer of the Dragon's Eye, the Dragon Master?"

"*Sssorrr!*"

"Will you also swear to help and assist his pupils, and to teach them those things that lie within your power?"

"*Sssorrr!*" Torcher's voice rang out more clearly with every utterance.

Now Dr. Drake took over once more, addressing the full-grown dragons. "Do you accept Torcher of Dragonsbrook among your number?" he asked.

All six roared their agreement as one: "*SSSSORRR!*"

"Then, Torcher of Dragonsbrook, let your flame be joined with the six!" boomed Dr. Drake triumphantly.

Seven jets of flame poured from the mouths of the dragons, making a fiery rainbow above Dr. Drake's head. He held the Dragon's Eye aloft once more and let it reflect the dragon firelight, so that it shone like a many-coloured star.

"Now that there are seven," Dr. Drake said, "which shall be the Guardian? Have you chosen?"

"The choice was made long ago," Brythonnia responded. "With the approval of the council, the old Guardian took on an apprentice to pass on the ways of her craft, so that when she died, her knowledge would not fail."

"Then let the apprentice step forth!"

Idraigir took a step towards Dr. Drake. He threw back his head and roared. It was a type of roar I had heard only once before: when the dying Guardian summoned all the dragons of the island of Britain to defend her. The sound seemed to come from his belly and shook the air around us. It was so loud that I felt sure it must have been heard far beyond the stone walls of the cavern.

"It is I!" he exclaimed. I could hardly believe this great honour was being bestowed upon a dragon we knew so well. I felt fidgety, wanting to clap, cheer, or holler *"Bravo!"* but the cavern remained deathly quiet as Dr. Drake continued, and I knew I must keep my excitement to myself.

"By which word do you claim the Guardianship?" he cried.

"By one previously secret that shall henceforth be known to you all! It is *CARDOCA-OCAR-OCARD!*" came Idraigir's reply.

"Do you swear to guard the solemn pact that was made between men and dragons over six hundred years ago?"

"*Sssssorrr!*" Idraigir gave an impressive roll to his *r*'s.

"Do you swear to protect both humans and dragons that they may live in peace?"

"*Sssssorr!*"

"Do you swear to safely guard the treasures distributed among the Seven Dragons and to be keeper of the Dragon's Eye?"

"*SSSSORRR!*"

With his questions to Idraigir now over, Dr. Drake turned to address the six dragons remaining—including little Torcher, who looked so serious it was almost comical.

"Dragons that came to grieve for the old Guardian, join us now to welcome the new!" cried Dr. Drake. "Dragons that came to grieve for dragons slain, join us to celebrate those that live!"

"*Sssssorrr! Sssssorrr! Sssssorrr!*"

"Members of the time-honoured Society of Dragons, by your teeth and your claws, by your horns and your hot dragon fire, do you abide by this judgement?"

"*Sssssorrr! Sssssorrr! Sssssorrr!*" they replied, giving a new lightness to their answer that relaxed us all and suggested that the ceremony would soon be at an end.

Finally, it was our turn, as Dr. Drake asked us: "Humans— members and students of the Secret and Ancient Society of Dragonologists—by your heads and your hands, by your wits and your wills, do you abide by this judgement?"

We shouted together with all our might, "We do! We do! We do!"

"Then, hail the Guardian Dragon!"

"Guardian Dragon, hail!" we chorused.

The ceremony was over, but my heart still pounded with the drama of it all.

CHAPTER THREE

THE DRAGONOLOGICAL DINNER

Send trusted men to infiltrate their councils in secrecy, so that the plots of the dragonologists shall be laid bare. Appearing to love dragons, you shall learn how dragondom may be brought low.

—— *Malleus Draconis (The Hammer of the Dragons), Edvardus Rex*

D r. Drake was still deep in conversation with the seven dragons in the Guardian's Chamber as Beatrice and I made our way through the tunnel with our parents. A fleet of carriages was waiting to take us on to that evening's Dragonological Dinner. I wanted to ask so many questions, but my head was spinning with the wonder of the ceremony, and instead I merely sat gazing out from the carriage at the darkening countryside around us until we arrived at a grand old house. By now night had fallen, and lights blazed in its every window.

"Goodness, where are we?" I asked as we rumbled along the driveway.

Father swept out his arm dramatically and announced, "Daniel and Beatrice, may I welcome you to Wantley Hall!" Then he laughed and began to explain our location. "The house is over one hundred years old and a beautiful example of Georgian architecture. We are here as the guests of General Sir Jacob Morely, an old friend of Lord Chiddingfold's and a long-standing member of the Society."

"Is that Sir Jacob?" asked Beatrice, pointing to a uniformed man who stood erect at the top of a grand stone staircase to the side of the imposing front door.

"No, that is Sir Jacob's butler," Father whispered, amused by my sister's mistake.

"Please don't point." Mother did not seem so lighthearted, however. "You know you really must mind your p's and q's when we get inside. This dinner is going to be quite a formal affair."

"What are the dragons going to do whilst we're eating?" I wondered aloud.

"They are having their own Dragon Dinner, I believe," Father replied.

Beatrice laughed. "Will they have to mind their p's and q's, too?"

"I'm sure they have their own set of rules when it comes to dining," Mother answered rather stiffly. She seemed a little nervous.

We felt like royalty, alighting from the carriage and ascending the stairs to announce ourselves to the butler. He did not utter a word but simply led the way into an ornate dining room, its walls lined with portraits of self-important-looking ladies and gentlemen. I guessed the paintings were of Sir Jacob's illustrious ancestors. Looking up, I saw that the ceiling was magnificently decorated. Vibrant paintings of Chinese *lung* dragons swirled around the enormous, twinkling chandelier that illuminated the room.

Beatrice and I searched for our names on the place cards set out on the long dining table. We were relieved to discover that we would be sitting with our friends Darcy Kemp and Billy and Alicia Light. I had worried what I might say to Lord Chiddingfold, or even Mr. Gladstone, had I been seated near either of them.

The table had been set, it seemed, for a meal of many courses. "Why do we need so much cutlery?" I complained. "And how will I know which glass to use?" I counted at least five knives, six spoons, and four forks at each place setting.

Beatrice sighed. "Just copy me," she said, sitting up in her seat in an attempt to make herself look superior. "I had to learn it all at school. You won't have to worry about the glasses, though. Most of them are for wine, and we'll just be drinking water."

Billy and Alicia soon joined us with Darcy, and we all sat chatting together excitedly. It wasn't long, however, before Alicia and Beatrice began whispering to each other secretively, as was their habit.

Billy raised his eyebrows. "Girls." He sighed, shaking his head.

The room was beginning to fill up, and I was amazed by just how many people were arriving. There were far more than had been at the ceremony.

"I never knew the S.A.S.D. had so many members," I marvelled, wondering whether this explained Mother's nervousness earlier. "Do you know any of them, Billy?" I asked.

"I know all of the famous ones," he answered matter-of-factly. "They've all been to Father's house at one time or another."

Alicia looked up from her conversation with Beatrice. "Don't get him started, please!" she begged. "Once he gets going, he just won't stop."

Billy looked hurt. "Nobody is asking your opinion, Alicia," he snapped, then turned in a huff towards Darcy and me. "See that chap in the checked jacket? He's Edison, the famous American inventor. His most famous idea is something called a phonograph. Dr. Drake wants to use it to try to record the sounds of dragons in the wild. Then he'd be able to listen to them whenever he liked, and they'd be excellent for use at the school."

At first I thought that Billy was making it up. "I can't see how you could ever keep a record of a sound unless you simply described it on paper," I scoffed. Then again, not so long ago, if someone had tried to tell me that dragons were real, I should have laughed out loud. "How on earth would this phonograph work, anyway?"

"Don't ask me. I haven't a clue!" Billy laughed. "Oh, but look who Father is talking to now!" he exclaimed.

Darcy and I exchanged blank looks.

"You mean you don't recognise him?" Billy was in his element. He had the perfect excuse to show off, and for once I didn't really mind. I'd never seen so many illustrious people, and I was glad to have a friend close by who could tell me who was who.

"*That* is Henry Morton Stanley," Billy continued.

"What, the explorer who found Dr. Livingstone in Africa? The one who said, 'Dr. Livingstone, I presume?'" I felt I had to prove to Billy that I wasn't a complete ignoramus.

"Of course it is, but that's not all he's famous for. I'll bet you didn't know that it was Stanley who suggested to Dr. Drake that Jamal's egg had probably come from the Ngoro Ngoro crater? He was really rather pleased when you flew Jamal back there and proved him right."

"Was he, indeed?" I smiled but couldn't help feeling a little annoyed. "Nobody ever tells us anything." I wasn't cross for long, though; the crowd was too distracting.

"Who's that man in the corner with the colourful necktie?" asked Darcy.

"Ah," said Billy importantly. "Now, *that* is Richard Owen. He's the founder of the Natural History Museum."

"Oh, yes, the one who came up with the word *dinosaur*."

I was confident Billy had not expected me to know that fact. I tried to hide a smug grin, but Darcy saw it and grinned back at me.

"That's the one!" Billy continued breezily. "He's helping Dr. Drake with some secret research on extinct dragons. They even discussed whether or not to exhibit dragon relics in the Natural History Museum. Mr. Owen was all for it, but Dr. Drake said that the time was not right."

"Do you think that's because of the attack on Brythonnia?" I was keen to get Billy's take on the situation. "I suppose you and Alicia must have heard all about it?"

"Alicia and I have *overheard* some things, but we haven't been told anything official yet." At least that was one thing we were both in the dark about. "There are a lot of rumours flying around, but all we know for sure is that both Brythonnia and Somerled have been attacked."

"Somerled has been attacked?" I was shocked. "We only heard about Brythonnia."

"Well, Somerled's all right, but Brythonnia is still very shaken up. It's something to do with a ring that was found near her lair. They found one that was identical near Somerled's lair as well."

"The Dragonsbane ring?" I asked. This time Billy took notice.

"Shhh! We're not supposed to say that word. And anyway, how on earth did you know about the ring?" he demanded.

"Oh, I like to keep my ears and eyes open," I answered

nonchalantly, secretly pleased that I'd finally impressed Billy.

"Of course," Billy went on, "Mr. Tibbs is saying it's all Dr. Drake's fault. He claims that the attacks are probably the work of Alexandra or Ignatius and says that Dr. Drake should have kept a better eye on them."

I noticed Beatrice and Alicia had broken away from their conversation at last and were listening to us. Beatrice looked indignant. "Only a year ago, Mr. Tibbs was sticking up for Ignatius and Alexandra," she said hotly. "He's impossible!"

"It certainly seems that Dr. Drake can't do anything right as far as Tibbs is concerned," I commented.

"Anyway, Ignatius *is* dead, isn't he?" Darcy remarked, raising his voice a little too much. The room was suddenly quiet, and I realised someone was standing right behind me. It was obviously someone important, as I saw Beatrice spring to her feet, then flop into a perfect curtsey.

I turned and discovered that the Prime Minister had been circling the table, greeting the guests. He was now standing right behind me. I scrambled quickly from my chair and made a low bow.

"Young man. Young miss," said Mr. Gladstone, looking directly at my sister and me. "We have not been introduced, but I take it that I have the honour of addressing Daniel and Beatrice Cook?"

Beatrice curtseyed again.

"And do you know who I am?"

"Yes, sir," we chorused. My cheeks were burning with embarrassment, but I felt unbelievably proud. Fancy the Prime Minister being "honoured" to meet *us*. That really *would* show Billy!

Mr. Gladstone smiled. "Then let me congratulate you on the splendid job you did helping to counteract the perils of that dreadful dragon plague," he continued. "If only this dragon business didn't have to be kept so secret. Under normal circumstances, such actions as yours would warrant prominent public recognition."

"Thank you, sir," I answered breathlessly.

The Prime Minister lowered his head towards us. "I wanted to let you know — in confidence, you understand — that the queen has heard all about your efforts, too. Her Majesty often asks in private how things are progressing in the dragon world. She cannot show her interest openly, but she has asked me to pass on her warmest regards to you both." Mr. Gladstone straightened up and spoke so that everyone could hear him. "How is that dragon chick you are looking after, by the way? What's his name again?"

"Torcher, sir," Beatrice replied.

"Ah, yes, Torcher, of course. I have seen him. He did very well during the Dragon Rite, didn't he? You've obviously both done a splendid job with him. Keep up the good work!"

"Thank you, sir," Beatrice answered graciously.

For a moment I found myself unable to speak. I tried to stammer out a thank you, but nothing came. Then all of a sudden I found my voice again, though I was hardly in control of the words that came next from my lips. "Excuse me, sir," I asked. "But do you mind if I ask you a question?"

"Of course not!" Mr. Gladstone answered, smiling.

"Do you think Dragonsbane has returned, sir?" I have no idea what made me say it aloud and in front of all the assembled dinner guests. There were gasps around the room. Mr. Gladstone's smile slipped from his face, and he stiffened visibly. Worst of all, from the corner of my eye, I caught a look of absolute horror on my mother's face.

At last, Mr. Gladstone relaxed a little and answered kindly, "Well, there have been some very unusual goings-on recently. Very unusual, indeed. But I think I had better leave any explanations — or theories — to the Dragon Master himself. He will say something about the matter in due course, I am sure."

The Prime Minister returned to his seat at the top of the table, just as the double doors behind him swung open and in marched Dr. Drake.

The butler's voice rang out across the crowded room: "Please be upstanding and raise your glasses for Dr. Ernest Drake, the Dragon Master of the Secret and Ancient Society of Dragonologists." As one, we rose from our seats and lifted our glasses.

Dr. Drake took his place between the Prime Minister and Lord Chiddingfold and picked up his glass.

"I offer a toast," he announced, "even in these times of

renewed danger, to the ancient pact between men and dragons. May it never be broken. And to Idraigir, the new Guardian!"

"To the ancient pact!" we repeated as we clinked glasses with our neighbours. "And to the new Guardian!"

"And now"—Dr. Drake smiled, relaxing at last—"let us sit and eat!"

I suddenly realised that I was ravenous, and I sat down eagerly, to be met with a steely look from Beatrice. "Daniel," she hissed, "we're not even supposed to know about Dragonsbane. How could you give us away like that?"

"I don't know," I said. "I couldn't help myself. It just came out. I'm sorry."

I turned to Billy, anxious to continue our earlier conversation.

"Do you know anything about the white dragon?" I asked.

"You mean Erasmus?" said Billy.

"Yes. Why is Erasmus white? Are frost dragons allowed to be members of the Society of Dragons?" Now that the serious issues of the day seemed to be over, I was eager for some answers.

"Erasmus is a half-breed," explained Billy. "His father is a frost dragon called Spitz, and his mother is Brythonnia."

"She's a European dragon, of course," added Alicia.

"Does that mean Erasmus migrates, like other frost dragons?" Beatrice asked.

"No, he lives here. He says that it's too cold for him at

the poles. But he's inherited his father's white scales, and he breathes frost rather than fire."

"Have you ever spoken to him?" I was fascinated.

"Oh, yes, but he's terribly high and mighty," Alicia replied. "Before he was summoned to the council, he spent most of his time avoiding humans altogether."

I opened my mouth to ask yet another question, but Billy gestured for me to be quiet. Servants were moving along the table with platters of roast beef.

"We don't know if the servants are in on the dragon thing," he whispered.

We waited as our plates were filled with delicious-smelling meat and ladled with gravy and steaming vegetables. Once the servants had gone, Billy held up a piece of beef so that it flopped limply from his fork. He smiled wickedly. "This is the kind of thing the dragons will be having for their dinner," he said. "Only it will probably be raw—and still kicking!"

"Ugh," said Alicia, pushing her plate away. "I'm not feeling at all hungry now."

"We were talking about Erasmus," I continued eagerly as I shovelled a large forkful of food greedily into my mouth.

"Well," said Billy, "what we can't understand is why Idraigir has chosen Erasmus to be his new apprentice."

Beatrice nearly choked on a mouthful of parsnip. "His apprentice?" she spluttered.

"Yes. Now that Idraigir has become Guardian, he has had to take on a successor to train: the Dragon's Apprentice.

Apparently, none of the other dragons wanted the job—they say that they are too old and set in their ways. So Erasmus was chosen, but I'm not so sure that's the full reason."

As soon as we had finished the meal, there came a tapping of knife against glass as Dr. Drake called for silence. When everyone finally stopped talking, he stood up.

"Would you all be so kind as to listen for a few moments?" he asked. "I am saddened to say that there are grave and disturbing goings-on in the dragon world at the moment. Here, today, we have more members of the Secret and Ancient Society gathered together than we have had for a great many years, and so I have agreed with our esteemed Prime Minister to take this opportunity to quash a few unfounded rumours and to explain our current situation."

Dr. Drake and Mr. Gladstone exchanged serious glances and nodded graciously to each other. "As many of you know," Dr. Drake continued, "there have been two cowardly attacks on members of the Society of Dragons. Neither attack succeeded, but in each case a ring was found marked with a very distinctive *D*-rune. I think most of you will understand what that means."

A murmur of voices rippled around the room, and I felt sure I heard the name Dragonsbane whispered more than once.

"Precisely," said Dr. Drake, having waited for his audience to settle down again. "Now that the threat has become known, we should indeed refer to them by name: Dragonsbane."

The audience gasped as one, but as the noise died down, a single chair scraped noisily across the polished floor. "Excuse me, but I really must beg to differ!" Mr. Tibbs was on his feet, and he looked quite angry. "Dragonsbane, indeed. Those deluded dragon slayers have been dead for hundreds of years. Whoever is making these attacks knows exactly where to strike, and I am afraid to say that I hold our dear Dragon Master here at least partly to blame."

Mr. Tibbs pointed accusingly at Dr. Drake. And now Lord Chiddingfold pushed back his chair and rose to his feet.

"Hang on a minute, Tibbs," he interrupted. "This is hardly the time or the place. I know that we don't always see eye to eye with Dr. Drake, but he's been right about a lot of things lately. How on earth do you conclude that any of this is his fault?"

"It is quite simple," replied Mr. Tibbs. "There is no need to reanimate long-dead enemies. There are two villains whom we *know* to be sworn enemies of the S.A.S.D. And both have slipped from the Society's clutches because of mistakes made by Dr. Ernest Drake."

"You are referring to Alexandra Gorynytchka and Ignatius Crook, I presume?" Lord Chiddingfold looked at Mr. Tibbs wearily.

"Might I be allowed to continue?" Dr. Drake suggested, unruffled by Mr. Tibbs's interruption.

Lord Chiddingfold nodded and took his seat once more. He gestured for Mr. Tibbs to do likewise, and eventually, with a ferocious scowl on his face, Tibbs sat down.

"Now," Dr. Drake continued, "it is true that the Russian dragonologist Alexandra Gorynytchka persistently evades capture."

"You are quite sure she did not die at Hong Wei?" Mr. Gladstone interjected.

"I am completely sure. Emery here has collated several reliable sightings — of Miss Gorynytchka in Norway; of her sidekick Shadwell in Paris; and of a large flock of Tunguska war dragons in northern Canada. I doubt that she is up to any good, but I would surmise that she has retreated to lick her wounds and rebuild the strength of her dragon army. A woman of Alexandra's conviction does not simply abandon her plans for world domination. She has the means to hypnotise dragons and, should she wish to kill them, she can do so much more effectively than with dynamite. These attacks are not her style. I cannot believe that she has any connection with them."

At this, another ripple of anxious chatter circled the dining room. I was listening with rapt attention, pleased that we were at last considered important enough to hear the truth.

Dr. Drake cleared his throat to continue, and the room fell silent once more. "Of course," he began, "I consider Miss Gorynytchka to be one of the gravest threats the S.A.S.D. has ever encountered. She is still in possession of several stolen treasures that the S.A.S.D. would very much like returned to the new Guardian."

"And what about Ignatius Crook?" Mr. Tibbs interrupted angrily. "Couldn't he be behind the attacks?"

"Ignatius Crook is dead," said Dr. Drake. Once again the room fell silent. Only Mr. Tibbs scoffed openly and muttered. He obviously didn't believe Dr. Drake.

"Dead?" exclaimed the Prime Minister at last. "How so?"

Dr. Drake went on to explain that Ignatius had had a plan to search for the Lost Island of Dragons. It seemed Crook had found what he was looking for; the island was apparently somewhere in the Atlantic. His partner in wickedness, a certain Captain Hezekiah, had taken Crook to the island but was later found, deranged and badly burned, in the smouldering remains of his ship as it washed up on the coast of Virginia. Of course, no one believed his story about dragons, but the press got hold of it, and their report came to the attention of American dragonologist—and good friend of Dr. Drake's—Noah Hayes. Noah visited Hezekiah just before he died.

"What did he find out?" asked Lord Chiddingfold.

"Very little," Dr. Drake continued, shaking his head. "All Hezekiah would say was that the island has its own powerful guardian—a huge amphithere, if his description can be trusted. He saw Ignatius Crook consumed by dragon fire whilst Hezekiah himself barely managed to escape in his own ship."

"But if the attacks on the British dragons were not carried out by Ignatius or Alexandra, then surely the information on where to find their lairs must have come from someone in this room!" exclaimed Mr. Gladstone.

Silence fell once more as the members cast their eyes about the room suspiciously. "Is there a traitor in our midst?" Lord Chiddingfold asked aloud, waving a fist in the air. "A member of Dragonsbane, perhaps?" At this suggestion, the dinner guests began chattering excitedly, their voices growing more raucous by the moment.

"Tommyrot!" Mr. Tibbs cried, his voice cutting through the din. "Don't listen to Drake's nonsense. Dragonsbane has not returned. There has to be a simpler explanation."

"Now is not the time for argument, Mr. Tibbs," cried Dr. Drake. There was a clatter of plates and cutlery as he banged his fist on the dinner table in front of him. "Let us honour the terms of our pact to conserve and protect dragons in their time of need. We shall send volunteers to watch the approaches to the caves of each of the seven dragons. We fear Dragonsbane may be anxious to repossess the ancient treasures, and we cannot let that happen. We shall take steps to protect the remaining treasures of the S.A.S.D. and to stop these attacks now, whoever is behind them!"

At that, a rousing cheer went up from the adults, whilst we children drummed our spoons on the table. Finally, the Dragonological Dinner drew to a close with a round of toasts. It had been a remarkable day, but the mood at the end of it was uneasy. We all feared for the dragon council and dreaded what might happen next.

Chapter Four

ERASMUS

Let not knights bandy sweet words with those who would
assist dragons, but name them as ye find them —— wolves!
Traitors to our quest —— and to our realm!
—— *Malleus Draconis (The Hammer of the Dragons), Edvardus Rex*

We returned to Dragonsbrook early the next day, and Beatrice and I headed straight for the little turret room. Dr. Drake had asked each of us to write up eyewitness accounts of the Dragon Rite whilst everything was still fresh in our minds, but I found it impossible to concentrate. By the afternoon, all I had produced were five rather insipid lines, and I could see from looking over Beatrice's shoulder that she had written about the same. We didn't need to say anything to each other. We knew that we were both pondering the same question: Would our parents take up Dr. Drake's call to help protect the dragons and join the S.A.S.D. volunteers? Neither of us could bring ourselves to broach the subject. It was late afternoon before Mother called up, "Beatrice? Daniel? Father and I have something we need to tell you."

In fact, they did not need to tell us anything at all.

"How long will you be gone?" Beatrice asked bravely, her eyes filling up with tears.

Mother put an arm around Beatrice's shoulders. "We don't know," she answered. Her own eyes were damp and full of concern.

Father cleared his throat. "Your mother and I have been asked to keep watch over the sea entrance to the lair of Tregeagle, the Cornish dragon," he explained. "We have to go; it is our duty."

"We could come with you!" cried Beatrice desperately. "We would do anything to help you, but please don't send us back to boarding school."

"We could act as lookouts," I agreed enthusiastically. "Or we could carry messages. Even Torcher could help."

But it was no use.

"I'm sorry, but it's out of the question." Father didn't want to look us in the eye at first, but then he raised his head and thumped his fist on a nearby table. "But we are certainly not sending you back to boarding school. Torcher needs someone to look after him."

"And what of you and Mother?" wailed Beatrice. "Who will look after you? It is going to be so dangerous, especially when you don't know who is attacking the dragons."

Father smoothed a hand over Beatrice's hair and smiled kindly. "Your mother and I will be perfectly safe," he said. "Dr. Drake won't let anything happen to us, and we'll take every precaution we can, but remember, it is the dragons that are in danger, not us. We swore an oath to protect and conserve them, and now they really need our help."

Mother smiled. "Anyway, we are only going to Cornwall this time, not India. And we've already made arrangements for you to stay here whilst we're away."

"What? All on our own?" I blurted before I'd thought things through properly. Far better to stay here alone than have to go to boring Uncle Algernon's, where we used to spend all our holidays!

Mother explained that we would be quite safe; they had made arrangements so they could be sure of it. Darcy was to come and stay. He would prepare meals for us and collect Torcher's meat from the butcher in Horsham. They would leave us money for any provisions we needed to buy, and they would telegram with news as soon as they could.

No sooner had Mother explained the plan than Dr. Drake arrived with a cart to carry their luggage. He glanced around.

"Has your guest not arrived yet?" he asked.

"You mean Darcy?" Beatrice asked, perplexed.

"Oh, no, no, not Darcy," Dr. Drake answered enigmatically.

"Is it Nia?" gasped Beatrice hopefully. Nia was the daughter of Noah Hayes, the dragonologist who had sent word from America of Ignatius's death. She and Beatrice had become great friends during our Indian adventure the year before. Beatrice was to be disappointed, however.

"I'm afraid it isn't Nia either," Dr. Drake replied. "Actually, I think I shall leave it as a surprise." His mouth twitched into a knowing smile. "Now remember, if you have any problems that you cannot deal with, there is always someone at S.A.S.D. headquarters who can get a message to me."

"What if it's Mr. Tibbs?" I asked, remembering Tibbs's sneering performance at the Dragonology Dinner.

"It might well be Mr. Tibbs. You know you really shouldn't let him worry you, children, but if you absolutely don't want to talk to him, Mr. Flyte can always pass on your message."

Dr. Drake refused to be drawn out further on the matter of the mysterious guest, and with the preparations for our parents' departure and the anxiety of saying good-bye, I almost forgot all about it. As soon as they had left, early that evening, Beatrice swiftly reminded me.

"I must say," she began, "I think it is rather mean of Dr. Drake to tell us to expect a guest and not let us know who it is."

"Actually, I think it's quite exciting." I grinned, imagining the possibilities. "But since we don't know who it is, we can't really prepare for him. So why don't we go and see what we can find out about Dragonsbane in Ebenezer Crook's *History of the S.A.S.D.* whilst we're waiting?"

Beatrice could think of nothing better to do, so I fetched the thick volume from Father's bookshelf and placed it on his work desk. I quickly thumbed through the pages to find the relevant entry.

"Look — here it is." Beatrice peered over my shoulder as I read, "*On the Founding of the Dragonsbane.*

"In 1279, the Earl of Northumberland, one of the crusader companions of King Edward I, led a raid on the lair of a European dragon named Alba who dwelt in the Cheviot Hills. The Earl was young and inexperienced in the ways of dragons, and he was not ready for Alba's fiery response: a series of deadly dragon attacks on Bamburgh Castle. Despite his best efforts, the Earl, unable to defeat Alba, was forced to call on King Edward I for assistance. The king —— who had a reputation as a first-rate dragon slayer after the model of Saint George —— narrowly escaped his attack on Alba with serious burns. Enraged at his own failure, he ordered the destruction of every dragon in the kingdom and, in 1281, founded the Secret Order of Dragonsbane Knights. This order was to be regulated by a book that he himself had written entitled *Malleus Draconis* —— 'The Hammer of the Dragons.' Each Dragonsbane Knight swore an oath that he would not rest until, like his patron, Saint George, he had rid the land of at least one dragon."

Beatrice gasped in horror. "That's monstrous," she cried. "But who on earth would want to carry on with the oath today?" I read on, leaving her question hanging in the air.

"From that time forth, the Order of Dragonsbane Knights carried out great slaughter among the dragons of Britain, for instead of ordinary weapons, they were able to wield certain more powerful weapons that Edward had acquired in Aleppo on his return journey from Palestine after the Ninth Crusade. These included the famous Dragon's Claw and the Spear of Saint George.

"They're both S.A.S.D. treasures!" I exclaimed. "So how did we come to acquire them from Dragonsbane? I wonder." Beatrice shrugged and took over reading the book.

"The Dragonsbane Knights used these weapons most cruelly, against both dragons and those dragonologists who studied and assisted them.

"Beatrice Croke and her son, Daniel, after their heroic flight to the court of Robert the Bruce, in Scotland, returned in secret to Wharncliffe, having formed the Secret and Ancient Society of Dragonologists with a number of other courageous dragonologists. A pact of mutual assistance was made between the intelligent dragons —— who had formed the Society of Dragons —— and the S.A.S.D. to resist the terror of the Dragonsbane Knights and, once their Order was at last defeated, to make sure that their evil actions could never again be repeated.

"The defeat of the Dragonsbane Knights came at the expense of the lives of many noble dragons and brave dragonologists. Several of the ancient weapons that they had used to harm dragons were captured by the S.A.S.D. Those that could be put to good purposes became the foundation of the twelve treasures of the S.A.S.D., whilst the most dangerous, such as numerous vials of deadly plague powder and —— the most evil of them all —— the mighty Hammer of the Dragons itself, were sealed in a cavern deep on the volcanic Isle of Dragons."

I looked up. "I knew that a lot of the treasures of the S.A.S.D. came from far away, but I never realised that so many of them were brought back by crusaders."

"Well, that certainly explains it," Beatrice murmured, thinking out loud. "And it explains something else, too."

I gave Beatrice a knowing look. "Why Ignatius Crook was so keen to find the lost Isle of Dragons," I said.

"Exactly," Beatrice agreed, closing the book with a resounding thump that sent a cloud of dust wafting into the air.

We both sat lost in our own thoughts for a moment, then Beatrice continued: "Brythonnia and Somerled are guardians of some of the treasures, aren't they?"

"Yes." I nodded. "Maybe Dragonsbane is trying to get them back so they can continue killing dragons!" I exclaimed, horrified at the thought.

"It's the obvious explanation," agreed Beatrice. "But if it's just the treasures they're after, then there is one good thing."

"Oh?" I said. I couldn't for the life of me think what Beatrice was talking about.

"Torcher," she cried. "They aren't going to attack him, because he doesn't have any treasures."

"I suppose not." I smiled.

"I hope they never get them back. I hope the S.A.S.D. is strong enough to protect them." Her eyes filled with tears once more. "And I pray that Mother and Father will be safe."

The next morning, Darcy arrived at Dragonsbrook with a cartload of meat for Torcher.

"You know, you're lucky," he began as we helped him unload the cart. "Lord Chiddingfold is so worried about Dragonsbane that he has taken Billy and Alicia out of school. He is making them stay indoors at his house in London under the watchful eye of Mr. Tibbs."

"Mr. Tibbs!" I exclaimed. "Poor Billy and Alicia. He'll probably spend the whole time moaning about Dr. Drake."

"You see?" Darcy laughed. "At least we are here with Torcher in the forest."

"Dr. Drake said we were going to have a guest," said Beatrice a little anxiously. "Do you know who it is?"

"Yes," Darcy admitted warily. "But don't get too excited. It's Erasmus. He's coming here to keep an eye on us all."

"The new Dragon's Apprentice?" I exclaimed.

"Yes, and, according to Billy, he's as disagreeable a dragon as you will ever meet. He's only coming to watch over us because Idraigir has insisted upon it. Apparently he goes on and on about how he doesn't like humans. We have to be especially careful how we speak to him, because he has a nasty temper."

"I bet they're exaggerating," I said hopefully.

"Well . . ." Darcy gave me a rueful look. "I can tell you one thing: he's going to hate being here if all the action is happening somewhere else."

"Perhaps Billy and Alicia are the lucky ones after all," said Beatrice, trying to laugh. "Erasmus sounds like the Mr. Tibbs of the dragon world."

"Well, *I'm* looking forward to meeting him, anyway," I announced huffily. Surely Erasmus couldn't be all that bad.

I did not have long to wait. After supper, as we sat discussing the day's events, there came a thunderous crash outside, followed by a rapid beating of wings and what sounded very like a string of loud Dragonish curses. We rushed to the window just in time to see Erasmus sitting on a pile of broken bricks, looking very disgruntled. It seemed he had misjudged the tight landing and crashed into a corner of the stable block. He continued cursing in Dragonish; translated into rather more polite English, he was probably saying something like, "Which wingless, harebrained human chose to position these confounded buildings in such a gloomy, overgrown wood, and what kind of half-wit would want to live in a stone hovel in such a hideous, inaccessible forest, anyway?"

Erasmus gazed about himself with great distaste, his white scales giving him the appearance of a ghost dragon in

the moonlight. Even Torcher, having heard the commotion, had come to see what was going on and was studying Erasmus with great curiosity.

"*Praisich boyar!*" I said eagerly as we rushed out of the house to greet the impressive-looking frost dragon. "Are you really here to protect us?"

Erasmus opened his mouth to speak, but then closed it again and turned away from me with a shudder.

"I saw you at the ceremony," I added. "Wasn't it wonderful?"

Still Erasmus did not say anything.

Beatrice let out a sigh. "Here we go," she whispered to Darcy and me. "Let me try." She gave a slight bow. "Welcome to Dragonsbrook, mighty Erasmus," she said. "We are both pleased and honoured that you have come to protect us."

Erasmus snorted, gazing off into the distance, and made a face to suggest that conversing with us was far beneath his dignity. Meanwhile Torcher was sniffing about. Suddenly, he looked at Erasmus with increased interest, as though he had only now recognised him from the ceremony and, presumably, the Dragon's Dinner afterwards, by his scent.

"*Praisich!*" he said "*Praisich!*"

"Oh, well done, Torcher!" exclaimed Beatrice, beaming at him. We had been trying to teach our little dragon to say hello in Dragonish for ages, and now that he had finally managed it, we wanted to give him plenty of attention and praise, by way of encouragement.

Erasmus, however, ignored Torcher. The little dragon couldn't understand how anyone could possibly resist him, so he leapt up underneath the white dragon's chin and just managed to butt him on the muzzle.

"Torcher, no!" I cried, trying to pull him away from the older dragon.

Erasmus gave a low growl but still refused to look down at Torcher. The little dragon tried butting Erasmus again.

"Torcher," Beatrice snapped sternly. "I don't think Erasmus wants to make friends just yet."

Erasmus sighed. Then, finally, he spoke. His voice was cold and distant.

"Have I not made it clear by my behaviour that I wish to be left in peace?" he spoke wearily, as though making an enormous effort. "It is true that I have been exiled here and it is my task to guard you, but I will find this process less painful if we simply ignore one another. Unfortunately, you must take lessons with me from first thing tomorrow morning. I shall be able to endure no more than half an hour a day. There will be twenty lessons in all. Please understand that I do this purely because it is my duty to the Society of Dragons; in no way are my teachings intended as a favour to you."

I wondered if Erasmus was always so long-winded, or whether he just liked to sound grand and important.

"Dr. Drake didn't say anything about lessons," I responded, a little uneasy at the thought. Erasmus snorted, and his reply came with a rising sense of anger and irritation.

"You are the boy who dares hope that he might one day become Dragon Master—the successor to the great Dr. Drake—are you not? Well, from what *I've* been told, you, my boy, are going to need to study a great deal harder before *that* is ever going to happen. For myself, I don't believe there should be another Dragon Master. Indeed, once I am Guardian, I shall break the pact made between dragons and humans over six hundred years ago. Far too many humans are aware of the existence of dragons, and they cause more problems than they solve. We don't need to be conserved and protected. We need to be forgotten!"

"But why should we break the pact?" asked Darcy, startled. "And how can you be the Dragon's Apprentice if you don't believe there should even be a pact?"

Erasmus sniffed and lifted his snout haughtily into the air. "Humans cannot be trusted. That can form the basis for our first lesson. Idraigir believes that spending time with you all will encourage me to change my mind. He is wrong; I will not. And now, please leave me alone! And take that half-tame, human-loving dragon chick with you! He should be catching wild deer in order to feast on their livers, not performing tricks in return for scraps from a butcher's shop."

"Torcher doesn't do tricks!" I began to protest, but Beatrice put her hand on my arm to stop me.

"We will leave you, Erasmus," she told the snooty dragon; I realised she was probably right not to get cross with him.

"Please don't trouble yourself on our account. You are far too great."

"You are correct," Erasmus answered seriously. "I am, in fact, both wise and great."

"Come on, Daniel and Darcy," said Beatrice with more than a hint of sarcasm in her voice. "Let us take our half-tame dragon chick and leave the wise and great Erasmus in peace. We shall ignore him as he asks."

However, as we were leaving, Torcher, who had been irritated by Erasmus's behaviour—even if he hadn't understood his speech—leapt up and nipped the white dragon on the chin.

"Torcher, no!" I cried. I was horrified but trying not to laugh at the same time.

Erasmus's proud expression quickly contorted into anger. The great dragon roared and belched out a spray of icy venom. The dragon chick was completely engulfed—and frozen solid.

Beatrice and I were stunned for a moment, then instinctively we rushed to Torcher's side. "Erasmus, how could you?" I shouted.

"Stop, you fools!" the frost dragon bellowed. "The chick is too cold. If you touch him, you will stick to him."

Even Beatrice found it difficult to remain calm. "You've killed him!" she cried.

"Nonsense," scoffed Erasmus. "I've merely prevented him from irritating me for a while. He will thaw out soon enough,

I assure you. And now, by the fanged jaws of all the proud knight slayers of old, leave me in peace! I will look after this chick and make sure that he is safe. I have instructions to give him lessons, too—though he has already learned one today!" Erasmus examined his claws and refused to look any of us in the eye.

"How can you expect us to leave Torcher with you after what you have done to him?" exclaimed Beatrice. "How can we trust you?"

"You have no choice but to take my word," snorted Erasmus. "Now go, before you witness the full power of my anger!"

"Very well." Beatrice turned to leave but then swung back to face Erasmus, her eyes almost as steely as his. "But just remember that we will be watching you." And with that, she turned her back on Erasmus and stalked into the cottage.

Darcy and I followed Beatrice inside, but it was hard to relax. Luckily, it was a clear, starry night, so we watched Erasmus and Torcher anxiously from the parlour window. After what seemed an age, the end of Torcher's tail began to twitch, jerkily at first, then, as his wings flexed stiffly, shards of ice slipped from his back, and his wings began to creak open. His neck twisted slowly from side to side, and finally he shook off the melting ice and stretched out his legs one by one. I imagined that Torcher would then run from Erasmus as fast as his little legs could carry him, but, to my horror, he strode straight up to the bigger dragon and stood glaring up at him. Erasmus did not look down.

"I hope he's not going to do anything stupid," I said nervously.

The chick gave a loud hiccup.

"Torcher, no!" exclaimed Beatrice. But of course, the little dragon couldn't see her. She twitched the parlour curtain and gestured at him frantically, but to no avail.

A spurt of flame shot out of Torcher's mouth and singed Erasmus's chin. The frost dragon looked down, and I held my breath, expecting to see his face contort once more in a terrible rage. Instead, he leaned forward and said something to Torcher that we could not hear. Then he stood up and, with Torcher trotting happily behind him, disappeared into the forest.

"Oh, no!" I cried in horror. "We've got to stop them!"

Darcy shook his head doubtfully. "I don't think that would be a good idea."

Beatrice bit her lip. "But how can we trust Erasmus?"

"Well," Darcy reminded us, "Dr. Drake and Idraigir trust him, don't they? I'm sure Erasmus is strong enough to look after Torcher."

"Well, *I* don't trust him!" Beatrice folded her arms defiantly. "How dare he come here, acting all high and mighty, saying he is going to protect us then blasting poor Torcher and dragging him off into the forest? I'm not sure I want to study dragonology at all, with creatures like him to contend with!"

I couldn't help feeling Beatrice was being a little hasty. "Erasmus must have known that freezing Torcher wouldn't harm him," I ventured.

Beatrice was appalled. "Why are you defending him?" she snapped. "Great and wise dragon, indeed; he's a monster!"

"I'm just saying he must have had a reason for doing what he did," I argued. "But I agree: we have to do something about Torcher."

"What can we do?" Beatrice threw up her hands in despair. "Except wait until they both come back."

But Erasmus and Torcher did not come back that evening. Reluctantly, we took ourselves off to bed without knowing where our dragon chick had gone. I slept very little. I worried about my parents and the perils they might be facing. I worried about Torcher and what Erasmus might do to him — and about anything else in the forest that could harm him. I tried to remind myself that Dr. Drake and Idraigir knew what they were doing; Erasmus had been chosen as the Dragon's Apprentice, after all — surely he couldn't be all that bad. But the one thing I couldn't understand was why Idraigir had chosen as his apprentice a dragon who wanted to break up the ancient pact between humans and dragons.

The next morning, from an upstairs window, I noticed

that Erasmus had returned to the space in front of the stables, but I could not see Torcher anywhere. I rushed downstairs to find Darcy and Beatrice finishing their breakfast. My sister looked as though she had not slept a wink all night, either.

"Any news of Torcher?" I asked them.

"Not so far." Beatrice was obviously still quite cross. "Come on — let's go and speak to Erasmus."

The three of us ventured outside together, trying our best not to appear nervous in front of Erasmus. The dragon turned towards us haughtily.

"Ah, there you are," he sneered. "You are late for your first lesson."

"What have you done with Torcher?" Beatrice demanded.

"That foolish creature is very well, thank you. You may go visit him after your instruction has finished, seeing as you are so keen on information about his well-being. I notice that you do not ask how Erasmus is this morning."

"We want to see Torcher now," said Beatrice, ignoring the dragon's comment.

Suddenly I spotted a wisp of something red and scaly. I bent to examine it.

"Dragon skin!" I exclaimed.

Beatrice gasped. "What have you done with him?" she cried, shooting an accusing glance at the haughty dragon. "I knew we should never have trusted you!" She began casting about to look for clues as to Torcher's whereabouts.

"I have not *done* anything with him," retorted Erasmus impatiently. "I have merely taught him a few lessons about how a proper *wild* dragon should behave. He is not a human's pet; he should be proud of his horns, teeth, and flame and use them wisely. I noticed that he was on the point of shedding his skin, and so I assisted him by clawing off the first part. He is now in the forest scratching the rest off himself."

"The forest!" exclaimed Beatrice. "You left him there alone?"

"We must find him. Dr. Drake promised that I could have Torcher's shed skin to make a pair of flameproof gloves!" I added, hurrying towards the trees.

"Wait!" Erasmus commanded. "How dare you suggest such a thing? You dragonologists think you know all about us. Well, let me tell you that shedding one's skin is a very private activity. Extraordinarily private. Afterwards, the skin in question should be buried so as not to attract unwanted attention. Torcher will return when he has finished, and that is that." It was apparent from Erasmus's expression that all discussion about Torcher had ended and that it was time to move on.

"Now it is time for your lesson," Erasmus began, without waiting for us to find a seat or rush inside to grab our notebooks. "The Dragon Master asked me to instruct you on the reasons some dragons are more intelligent than others. Being half frost dragon and half European dragon—both very intelligent species—I, of course, am a good example of a dragon with highly superior intelligence. I would say that I have inherited brilliance from each side of my dragon ancestry and am therefore twice as intelligent as any creature that is merely the product of a single dragon species."

"I don't quite see how that works," Darcy began. We were all trying to settle on the grass in front of Erasmus but were finding that the nettles and stray branches of brambles made our positions rather uncomfortable.

"I would have thought that it was obvious," Erasmus boasted, completely ignoring our fidgeting.

"Is it because you use twice as many words to say everything?" asked Beatrice as she shuffled around to find a clear patch of grass. I couldn't help thinking how quickly her respect for our new visitor had evaporated.

Erasmus seemed to miss her sarcasm. "Well, of course, I have always been blessed with a large word hoard," he said proudly. "And language is an important indicator of intelligence."

Erasmus might have chosen a wide variety of words, but his speaking voice was dull and monotonous. I was so tired from the night before that I struggled to concentrate on what he was saying, even though I would have usually listened with unwavering attention to almost any discourse from a dragon.

"We may group the different species of dragons into those that can speak and those that cannot," he droned. "Knuckers, for example, have no speech, whilst European dragons, gargouilles, and *lung* have all mastered language."

I stifled a yawn, but a prick from a stray bramble startled me awake. "The roots of dragon language go far back into the mists of time," Erasmus continued, a little mysteriously. "Dragon language began long before any human tongue developed. Unlike humans, the different species of dragons around the world all speak a variety of the same basic language: Dragonish. Although most dragons tend to keep within their own species, sharing a common tongue means that they can communicate with another species when required."

"But why did dragons want to speak human languages in the first place?" asked Darcy.

"You tell me," Erasmus snapped suddenly.

"Um, was it so we could find out about them?" Beatrice suggested.

"Maybe," the dragon answered distractedly.

"Or was it because they wanted to find out about us?" At least speaking helped me to pay attention.

"A few dragons have learned human languages in order to share their knowledge with humans and to learn from them, but they much prefer beautiful, learned languages such as Latin, Greek, Sanskrit, and Mandarin Chinese to your barbaric tongue."

"So how has it happened that many British dragons do speak our 'barbaric tongue'?" I asked. Erasmus could be so vexing.

"Ah, that was all due to the Dragonsbane Knights," Erasmus explained, warming a little to the topic. "An adult human cannot learn a language as quickly as a dragon, and when Beatrice and Daniel Croke became involved with the dragon cause, our ancestors felt it important to speak a language the Crokes would clearly understand," Erasmus told us. "Of course, had the dragons been able to defeat Dragonsbane without the pact, they would not have needed to learn English, and I would not have to give you this lesson," he snapped, and was then silent for a few moments.

"But why couldn't the dragons defeat Edward's knights on their own?" I prodded, starting to warm to the subject myself. "Why did they need the help of Beatrice and Daniel?"

"The weapons King Edward brought back from the Ninth Crusade were too powerful," Erasmus explained with reasonable patience. "Once upon a time, a fight between a knight and a dragon was a noble matter in which the knight stood practically no chance of killing the dragon. But once those cursed weapons were brought into play, everything changed. That is why the first Guardian sought the help of Beatrice Croke. We needed humans to understand the human world. Together they forged the ideals of the pact." He suddenly turned, and his eyes darted beadily from me to Beatrice, and then to Darcy. "And those ideals are . . . ?" he demanded.

"Er, that dragons should be protected and conserved by humans," Darcy began.

"That dragons and humans must never kill one another," Beatrice continued confidently.

"And that erring humans should face human justice, whilst erring dragons should always face dragon justice," I finished, feeling pleased that we had answered without hesitation.

"Indeed," said Erasmus. He seemed disappointed that we had been able to answer him at all.

"Do *you* think that Dragonsbane is trying to get their weapons back?" I asked.

"That is exactly what they are trying to do, which is why I cannot understand why I am not taking part in the conflict. What were Dr. Drake and Idraigir thinking by sending me here?" Erasmus was starting to sound quite prickly again, but he seemed almost to be talking to himself.

"Perhaps in sending you here to spend time with us, Idraigir wants you to see that humans aren't as bad as you think," Beatrice suggested.

"In that case, he has failed miserably," Erasmus bellowed suddenly, startling us all. "After seeing the way you have treated that poor dragon chick —"

"What do you mean?" Beatrice interjected hotly.

Erasmus opened his claw and, to my horror, let two small stone objects fall to the ground.

"Just look at these!" He was indignant.

"Aren't those flint and iron pyrites?" asked Darcy.

"Yes, and look, they're the exact same stones you gave to Torcher," Beatrice said to me, then narrowed her eyes as she turned to address Erasmus. "Did Torcher give them to you willingly?" she demanded.

"No. Of course not," sniffed Erasmus unapologetically. "I was forced to take them from him." He paused and looked down accusingly at Beatrice. "That chick is far too young to be breathing fire. He can't be expected to use it wisely."

This was all too much for Beatrice. "I've heard enough," she cried. "I'm going to look for Torcher right now!" And with that, she stomped off towards the woods.

"Wait!" Erasmus commanded. I was surprised to see Beatrice stop in her tracks. "I expect the chick will have shed the rest of his skin by now. I will take you to find him. Daniel, keep the pieces of flint and iron pyrites until Torcher reaches proper fire-breathing age. I will let you know when that is."

I pocketed the two stones, and we all followed the frost dragon into the woods. But when Erasmus reached the place where Torcher should have been, there was no sign of him. Even Erasmus looked puzzled. Then he indicated a patch of freshly dug ground, prodded it with his claw, and brought up several pieces of red, scaly skin.

"So he *was* here," Beatrice said, panic rising in her voice. "But where has he gone now?"

"Well," said Erasmus, "it is true that he was in something of a temper when he ran from me. He has probably gone somewhere to calm down."

"On his own? In the forest?" exclaimed Beatrice. Her patience with Erasmus was at the breaking point.

"Perhaps he has gone to try to find more pieces of flint and iron pyrites, which he will have a job doing around here." Even Darcy was getting a little tight-lipped.

Beatrice finally snapped. She turned to Erasmus with a face like thunder. "You have no idea where he is, have you?" she raged.

"I do not," Erasmus replied. He seemed completely untroubled by either Torcher's disappearance or Beatrice's outburst.

"And you are supposed to be protecting him," Beatrice continued, marching towards him, her finger pointing accusingly in his direction. "And now he is roaming St. Leonard's Forest, unable to protect himself!"

Erasmus looked away. Was it possible that he felt embarrassed?

CHAPTER FIVE

MISSING

Steal the eggs from a mother dragon, and you will be
handsomely rewarded. But bring a live chick to bait,
and your reward will be far greater.

—— *Malleus Draconis (The Hammer of the Dragons), Edvardus Rex*

Come on, Erasmus! You've got to keep up!" cried
Beatrice.

"Wither and blast these overgrown weeds," cried Erasmus. He had become caught up in tree branches for the fourth time and was trying to wriggle his huge body through another group of birch trees. At twenty feet in length, Erasmus was still not fully grown. His large wings folded awkwardly into his body, making it difficult for him to advance through the dense forest. "My icy blasts are useless here. If only I could breathe fire, then I could burn my way through this jungle!" he exclaimed. "A forest is no place for a dragon such as I."

Finding it hard to sympathise with Erasmus, I ignored his complaints and focused all my efforts on searching for Torcher. "Can you still smell his scent?" I asked.

Erasmus snaked his long neck through the trees, sniffing the ground as he did so.

"You need a dog for a task like this, not a dragon," he grumbled.

"I thought dragons had a much better sense of smell than dogs," I retorted. We were all still furious with Erasmus.

"Wait!" The frost dragon bent down and sniffed the ground once more. "I am perplexed. The Guardian did not tell me anything about another dragon in the forest. But there is a second dragon's scent here."

"It could be Weasel," I said. "She's a knucker dragon."

"I don't mean a knucker," said Erasmus. "I would barely count those creatures as dragons. Torcher headed north. Could he have been fleeing a pursuer?"

"A pursuer?" snapped Beatrice, horrified. "What have you smelled? Tell us!"

"Dr. Drake didn't say that there was a basilisk here in the forest, did he?"

"A basilisk?" I trembled. I had encountered such a dragon only once before. Basilisks were deadly shape-shifters with insatiable appetites that caused them to prey upon virtually any creature they came across.

"Those cunning creatures might be able to hide their shape, but they cannot disguise their smell." Erasmus kept his muzzle to the ground. "At least not from me. They are extremely rare, but this tangle of twisted oaks is the perfect basilisk habitat."

"There wasn't a basilisk here before," Darcy said. "Dr. Drake would have identified it at once. It must have come here from somewhere else, and quite recently."

"But surely Torcher should be safe. Dragons don't prey on one another — do they?" Beatrice shuddered.

"Why on earth not? A hungry basilisk will eat practically anything," said Erasmus. "And Torcher will be an easy snack now that he has just shed his old skin. The basilisk won't even have to shell him."

"How can you say that?" Beatrice let out a desperate sob; I could feel tears pricking at my own eyes, too. "He can't even defend himself with fire now, thanks to you!" she continued.

"I am sorry. But I don't see how I am to blame," Erasmus answered. "I could not allow such a young dragon to breathe fire. It is hardly *my* fault that he became upset about it and ran away."

"You promised to look after him!" Beatrice scolded. "You should *never* have let him go."

"Perhaps not." Erasmus considered the situation for a moment, then continued casually, "But let us not give up hope until we really have to. We will search for him — or for his remains, at least — but we must be careful. I, of course, might be an equal match for most basilisk dragons — though I could still fall prey to its venomous bite and hypnotic stare. You children would simply make three very sparse mouthfuls."

I grabbed Beatrice's hand.

"We *must* find Torcher," I urged. She nodded, unable to speak for worrying.

"Now we shall continue searching to the north," said Erasmus, ignoring our anxiety. "But we would travel much more quickly through the air than through these unmentionable trees."

"Can you carry three of us?" I asked.

"Ugh!" Erasmus shuddered visibly. "I have always made it a rule never to fly with humans, but I suppose on this occasion I will have to make an exception. I shall not carry more than two of you, however."

"You two continue the search, and I'll return to the house," volunteered Darcy. "Torcher might come back by himself, and if he does, someone will need to be there to meet him."

"But what if the basilisk comes?" I worried.

"Oh, I'll be all right. But if there's any trouble, I shall blow three quick blasts on a dragon whistle. Erasmus, you'll be able to hear that, won't you?"

The dragon gave a halfhearted nod in Darcy's direction, then Beatrice and I climbed onto his back and he sprang into the air. Unused to carrying passengers, he lurched from side to side until I feared we would fall. Soon, however, we were flying northwards above the trees with at least some semblance of grace.

"By all the fiery dragons of Erebus!" grumbled Erasmus.

"You two are a weight and no mistake. You will have to consume rather less food in future if I am ever to consider letting you fly on my back again."

The tops of the forest trees stretched ahead of us for several miles, but far in the distance I could just make out a tall tower on a hill, perhaps four miles away. It had a strange kind of pole on the top of it, with three short arms branching from it.

"What's that building?" I pointed it out to Beatrice.

Much to my surprise, she knew. "It's a semaphore tower," she explained. "The navy used to use them to send coded messages from the coast all the way up to London."

I looked back down at the forest beneath us. The ground seemed far away now, too. "Can you still follow Torcher's trail from up here?" I shouted to Erasmus.

"Pah, it's easier to follow up here than on the ground," the dragon called back. "Unfortunately, so is the scent of the basilisk." I turned to look at Beatrice, who sat behind me clinging onto my waist. She returned an anxious grimace.

Presently, Erasmus began to circle around. There was some sort of clearing below us.

"Both trails end down there," he said.

"Both of them?" Beatrice cried. I felt her grip around my waist tighten.

"I am going to land," Erasmus announced. "Then we will try to see what is happening."

As soon as Beatrice and I dismounted, we began

searching for dragon tracks. At one end of the clearing, I found a large patch of brambles that had been torn and trampled.

"Maybe there was a fight here," I suggested.

Erasmus cast me an incredulous look. "If there was, then it wouldn't have been much of one. We should not forget, of course, that it is possible Torcher accompanied the basilisk willingly."

"Don't be ridiculous!" I retorted. "Torcher would have been terrified."

"I should have thought, with all your dragonological knowedge, you would be aware that basilisks are known for their animal cunning," Erasmus said. "It is possible that this one had just eaten and wanted to save Torcher for later. In that case it might have taken on a form that Torcher would find friendly — perhaps the shape of another dragon chick. True, it could not have disguised its smell, but then, as soon as Torcher locked eyes with it, the chick would have been hypnotised: fatal."

"Stop it!" cried Beatrice. "Don't talk about Torcher as if . . . as if . . ."

Erasmus looked surprised. "As if what?" he asked.

"As if he's already dead!" she shouted.

Erasmus didn't have a chance to reply, however, for I had spotted something — a possible clue to Torcher's whereabouts.

"A tunnel!" I cried. "It leads underground."

Erasmus sauntered over and sniffed at the tunnel entrance.

"Yes," he confirmed. "They went in here."

The hairs on the back of my neck stood up as I peered into the darkness. "Could this be the basilisk's lair?" I asked.

"Not if this basilisk has only just moved here. It would take even a determined dragon some time to dig out a lair this large," replied Erasmus, making me feel foolish once again. He lifted his muzzle and sniffed the air. "I suspect from the faintness of the smell that the imminent danger has passed."

"What do you mean by that?" Beatrice asked, bewildered.

"What is certain is that the trails only go in. Neither Torcher nor the basilisk came out this way again. So, unless the tunnel is very deep and they are still inside, there must be another exit."

"Does that mean we must all go through it to other side?" I asked.

"Not all of us." Erasmus let out an impatient sigh. "I am far too big to enter the tunnel," he snapped.

"Then Daniel and I will investigate," Beatrice told him. I was pleased that she now seemed far more determined than anxious. "But we're going to need some sort of light; it's so dark in there."

Erasmus made a noise as though he was clearing his throat, "Ahem. Fire is not my strong point." He said it quietly, almost under his breath. I wondered whether he might be jealous of Torcher's fire-breathing ability, but now was not the time to mention it.

I fumbled in my pocket for a moment and pulled out the stump of a candle. "I've got this," I said. "But I don't have any matches."

Beatrice snapped her fingers. "Try your other pocket!" she said. "Don't you have Torcher's stones?"

I dug my hand deep inside and found the flint and iron pyrites together with a good deal of pocket fluff that would act as perfect tinder. I soon got a small flame going and lit the candle.

The tunnel was damp with soft mud. Beatrice and I had to stoop as we stepped inside. Holding out my candle, I could just make out *two* sets of dragon tracks that disappeared into the darkness.

"Erasmus was right!" I exclaimed.

"About what?" asked Beatrice.

"The two sets of prints are identical. The basilisk must be copying Torcher's shape." I crouched down and held the candle close to the ground. The dragons must have brought foliage from the forest into the tunnel with them, stuck to their feet, for there were a number of leaves scattered around.

"Can you tell the two sets apart at all?" asked Beatrice.

I leaned closer to the ground. "I'm not sure, but one set of prints seems to have caused the leaves underneath to

wither; the other hasn't. Basilisk venom is deadly, isn't it? Do you think it might ooze out through their feet?"

"Wait a moment," Beatrice exclaimed, forgetting my question. She bent down to pick something up from the ground. "What do you make of this?"

Beatrice picked up a ring, rubbed at the mud that covered it, and held it up to the candlelight. It began to shine.

I trembled. "It looks like gold," I said. "Does it have any writing on it?" I could not bring myself to say what I was thinking.

"Yes," answered Beatrice. She swallowed and narrowed her eyes, turning the ring over and over in her hands. "It has a *D*-rune on it," she whispered. "And there's some writing around the edge."

"Can you read it?" my voice quavered.

"It's in tiny script; I think it's French." Beatrice held the ring closer to the candle. "It says, *'Mort aux Dragons'* — 'Death to Dragons.'"

"But that's horrible!" I gasped. "It's a Dragonsbane ring, isn't it? So they've come for Torcher after all."

Beatrice's eyes widened. "How could Dragonsbane have any connection with a basilisk?"

"I don't know," I said, "but we've got to find out. Come on!"

As we followed the tracks deeper into the tunnel, the passage became gradually narrower and lower. The candle flickered. I hoped desperately that it would last us until we found a way out, but already it was beginning to dim. After some time, the tunnel forked into two paths. One route seemed completely dark, but at the end of the other, a chink of daylight lit the way ahead. I scoured the ground for tracks and found fragments of old clay pipes and broken bottles. "It looks like a knucker hole," I told Beatrice, "judging from the debris left behind."

"Maybe it belonged to one of Weasel's ancestors," she suggested.

The tracks were less distinct now, but, to my relief, they followed the tunnel that led out of the ground. And there seemed still to be two sets.

"At least we know Torcher left with the basilisk," I said, breathing a sigh of relief.

We emerged into the sunlight at the foot of a small hill. "Where on earth are we?" I wondered out loud.

Beatrice pointed up the hill. "Look!" she said.

In front of us was the semaphore tower. A broad track swept westward to join the main road farther on.

"Let's call Erasmus," I said, suddenly relieved to know that he was nearby and could protect us.

Beatrice held up her dragon whistle. It had been given to her by the Master of Hong Wei. She took a deep breath and blew a long, high-pitched note. I could barely hear it, but to Erasmus it must have sounded loud and clear. Before long, he was swooping towards us, and for once I was actually pleased to see him.

When the frost dragon saw the ring, he instantly let out a roar so loud and savage that both Beatrice and I had to cover our ears. I prayed that no one else had heard.

Erasmus was quiet for a moment, then he spoke, almost breathlessly, and with passion. "The sight of rings such as this once struck fear into the hearts of many noble dragons," he cried. "I would recognise the form of that unspeakable *D*-rune anywhere. It is the mark of Dragonsbane." Erasmus paused to compose himself. "Had we arrived just a short while earlier, then I might have had a chance to make those scoundrels pay for their wickedness!"

"But what was the ring doing in the tunnel?" asked Beatrice.

"I do not know," said Erasmus bitterly. "But whoever left it there is up to no good. 'Death to Dragons' is their wretched motto, but I say death to Dragonsbane!"

CHAPTER SIX

WYVERN WAY

There are certain secret signs we have uncovered
that are used by those who would succour dragons.
Learn them well, for so shall ye gain their trust.

—— *Malleus Draconis, (The Hammer of the Dragons), Edvardus Rex*

U p in the air once again, Erasmus flew over a small
church and a cluster of houses, following the scent trail
that Torcher and the basilisk had left behind them. "Which
village is that?" I asked.

"It's either Faygate or Colgate," replied Beatrice, leaning
out to see across the frost dragon's wing.

"Do you think Torcher has come this far? Could he have
left the forest altogether?" I did not imagine two small dragons
would cover much ground, but Beatrice was more realistic.

"I suppose the basilisk could turn itself into a much
larger creature—a wyvern, perhaps—in order to move more
swiftly. Torcher might have travelled on its back."

I couldn't begin to imagine what kind of torture our
chick was experiencing.

We flew northwards, and the pattern of scattered villages and hamlets below us grew into larger and larger towns that eventually joined to become the vast, smoky sprawl of outer London. Erasmus did his best to fly over woods and common land. Then, upon reaching the River Thames, he landed in a large area of parkland, where we dismounted. Erasmus turned to address us.

"The scent trails turn here and follow the course of the river downstream." His tone was no longer cold and unfriendly as it had been the previous day.

"They've gone into the centre of London?" Beatrice gasped in disbelief.

"Yes. The two trails are both still fresh." Erasmus seemed almost concerned. "The dragons cannot be far in front of us. If we move swiftly, there is a very good chance that we might catch them."

"And then what?" I was starting to feel that our task was impossible. "You can't fight a basilisk in broad daylight in front of the Houses of Parliament."

"But I could continue the search after nightfall," Erasmus suggested helpfully, though he still did not seem to understand the urgency of the matter.

"We cannot wait until nightfall," I spluttered. "We need to find Torcher now!"

"And anyway," Beatrice interjected, "you can no more visit the Tower of London in the daytime than Torcher and the basilisk can stroll down Oxford Street!"

"Precisely," I agreed, but Beatrice's words had put a thought in my head. "Dragons cannot venture out in public during daylight hours, so Torcher and the basilisk must be hiding somewhere—lying low."

"Yes," mused Beatrice. "But we're going to need help to find them."

"Then I think we need to let the S.A.S.D. know what has happened," I announced. "It's time we asked for help."

"Hmm, Daniel is right," Beatrice agreed with me, and despite the situation, I couldn't help a triumphant smile. "I spotted a railway station just before we landed. It must be over in that direction." She pointed back the way we had come.

"No time to lose." We turned and began heading back towards the station.

"And meanwhile, what do you want me to do?" Erasmus called after us. "Return to the forest?"

"It would be most useful if you could make sure that Torcher hasn't left London," suggested Beatrice, hurriedly looking back at him over her shoulder. "Do you think that you could fly around the edge of the city without being seen?"

"I could," Erasmus answered. He sounded sulky now, but at least he hadn't said no.

"Good." Beatrice didn't give him a chance to change his mind. "See if you can detect his scent leaving the city anywhere. We will meet you at Dragonsbrook as soon as we can. If you discover anything, ask Darcy to get a message to us at the S.A.S.D. headquarters." We hurried on our way.

Catching a train into London was quite straightforward, and a little after two o'clock, Beatrice and I arrived at Dr. Drake's Dragonalia, the shop in Wyvern Way that hid the secret headquarters of the S.A.S.D. in its basement. We knew that Mr. Tibbs, Lord Chiddingfold's private secretary, would be there, but as neither of us liked him much, our plan was to speak to Mr. Flyte, who looked after the shop on the ground floor.

Unfortunately, Mr. Flyte had two customers with him, a man and a woman; they were arguing about whether to purchase an engraved jade box or one with a lacquer finish. I did not recognise either of them. I tried making the Sign of the Dragonological Apprentice to test the water, but they did not respond. It was clear that they were not members of the S.A.S.D. and we should not speak openly about dragons in front of them.

"Good morning, children," said Mr. Flyte cheerfully as he steered us behind the counter. "Mr. Tibbs is downstairs. If you are here on urgent business, you had better deal with him directly, though I should warn you that he is not in a very agreeable mood."

Beatrice and I warily descended the stairs that led to the S.A.S.D. headquarters.

"Is Mr. Tibbs ever in an agreeable mood?" whispered Beatrice.

"Perhaps we should wait and speak to Mr. Flyte," I

suggested, feeling a little fainthearted at the prospect of Tibbs and his temper.

"But this is urgent, Daniel," Beatrice reminded me. "Mr. Flyte would have to pass on our message to Mr. Tibbs, anyway. And I'm not going to let Tibbs's ill temper put me off." I knew she was right, but I still dreaded having to talk to the man.

The door to Mr. Tibbs's office was ajar, and a light shone out from inside. We knocked, but there was no reply.

"I wonder where he's gone." Beatrice was peering round the door. "Maybe he's in the Dragon Master's Office," I suggested, and began walking along the corridor. Beatrice followed, giving just a passing glance to the portraits of previous Dragon Masters that lined the walls.

The Dragon Master's Office was locked, but the door opposite was open.

We called out Mr. Tibbs's name and knocked, but there was no answer. I looked inside. The room was amazing, filled with glass display cases, lecterns, and plinths. I recognised at once some of the treasures they held. In a case by the door was a distinctive box that I knew to contain a silver tray loaded with dragon dust — a rare and precious substance, most valuable to any dragonologist. Beatrice and I had used some to counter the charm Ignatius Crook had cast upon Idraigir the first time we had seen Torcher's egg.

In the next case was a lectern with an open book resting on it. It was *Liber Draconis;* we knew it well. Its pages remained blank until brought to life by dragon fire. We could not have succeeded on our mission to save the naga dragons without it.

The Dragon's Eye, priceless symbol of the Dragon Masters, sat on a small cushion of red silk on a plinth opposite. Not long after we had met Dr. Drake, he had rescued the beautiful gem from the clutches of the dreaded Ignatius Crook.

I was so lost in thought that at first I did not notice Mr. Tibbs standing in the centre of the room with his back to us. I was just about to say hello when Beatrice grabbed my arm and pointed to a display case immediately ahead of him. I gasped, for there on a shelf were three treasures I had believed still to be in the possession of Alexandra Gorynytchka: Saint Gilbert's Horn, which could be used to summon or tame dragons; Splatterfax, the amulet that could reputedly call down a hail of rocks; and the Spear of Saint George, one of the few weapons capable of slaying a dragon outright.

"You've got them back!" I exclaimed.

Mr. Tibbs nearly jumped out of his skin. He spun round to look at us with a surprised expression on his face that quickly turned to one of horror as he recognised us. In his hand was the full-size, golden claw of a Chinese *lung* dragon. The five-toed talon clutched an enormous, sparkling diamond. I gawped at it, unable to speak for a moment. Although I had not seen it before, I knew at once that this must be the treasure known simply as the Dragon's Claw.

"But I thought Dragonsbane was after the S.A.S.D.'s treasures!" I exclaimed. "So how come you've got them all here safe and sound?" I pointed around the room.

Tibbs gave a harsh laugh that made me feel foolish. "You can't think that the S.A.S.D. would keep the *real* treasures here, surely? These are replicas, used purely for the instruction of advanced dragonologists. Dragons guard the real ones jealously, as you well know; they rarely let them out of their sight."

"Yes, of course," I replied a bit sheepishly.

"Mr. Tibbs, something terrible has happened," Beatrice blurted out.

"Why does that not surprise me?" Tibbs answered, his eyes narrowing. "What have you done now?"

"We haven't done anything," I protested. "It's Torcher. He's gone missing."

"So you *have* done something!" Tibbs gave a loud tut and shook his head as if in disbelief. "I knew that leaving you two alone in the forest would result in disaster. You should have gone to stay at Lord Chiddingfold's with Billy and Alicia as I suggested." In a flash of rage he added, "How on earth did you manage to lose the chick?"

"Well, Erasmus made him give up the pieces of flint and iron that he keeps in his spark pouch—" I began.

"And then Torcher got upset and ran away," Beatrice finished.

Mr. Tibbs gave us each a piercing stare. "But I thought

that Torcher was entrusted to *your* care, not to that of some overgrown adolescent dragon." He was almost snarling. "And so I suppose that now you want the entire Secret and Ancient Society to halt its efforts to protect all other dragons in order to hunt for a silly little chick that *you* should have looked after?"

Mr. Tibbs replaced the Dragon's Claw on its shelf. "So tell me," he asked, his anger fading slightly. "Where exactly did you lose Torcher?"

"He wandered off after shedding his skin," I explained.

"Yes, Erasmus was following his scent," Beatrice added earnestly. "We were all looking for him in the forest, then we came across a tunnel and inside it we found this. . . ."

She pulled out the ring and held it up for Mr. Tibbs to see.

"What?" He looked stunned for a moment, then snatched the ring from Beatrice and studied it carefully. "Has anyone else seen it?" he asked.

Beatrice shook her head. "Apart from Erasmus, no one," she answered.

"But there is something else you should know," I interrupted, then I paused for a moment to make sure I had Tibbs's attention and announced, "Torcher is travelling with a basilisk."

"With a what?" Mr. Tibbs spluttered. "A basilisk? Are you sure?"

"Erasmus told us that the scent was unmistakable. That's why we came here. We were following their trail, and it seems the basilisk brought Torcher to London."

Mr. Tibbs scratched his head. "A basilisk has brought Torcher to London, eh? So that is what Erasmus said, is it? A basilisk, hmm . . . ? In St. Leonard's Forest . . . and then London . . ." Suddenly he threw back his head and laughed out loud.

"I've got it!" he said, snapping his fingers. "Oh, ha, ha, ha! Most amusing! You have brightened up a dull day after all. Ha, ha, ha!"

"But I don't understand," Beatrice frowned. "*What* is so amusing?"

"Don't you see?" Mr. Tibbs made a visible effort to collect himself. "There can't be a basilisk in St. Leonard's Forest. Don't you see? Erasmus is making you the butt of a rather mean dragon joke. It is his revenge on Dr. Drake for making him instruct you in dragonology. And do you know why he would do such a thing?" Mr. Tibbs began to shake with laughter once more. "It's because Erasmus *really* hates children."

Beatrice and I looked at each other but said nothing.

Tibbs guffawed again. "Ha! A basilisk? In St. Leonard's Forest. The home of Dr. Drake. Oh, dear me, the very idea."

"But what about the ring?" I demanded. "How did that end up in St. Leonard's Forest?"

Mr. Tibbs waved his hand dismissively. "Oh, I expect Erasmus planted the ring so that you would assume the Dragonsbane Knights had struck again!"

"But Erasmus couldn't get to the part of the tunnel where we found it," I said coldly.

"And what about Torcher?" Beatrice demanded. "What would he do with Torcher?"

"I am sure that Torcher is perfectly safe and sound and getting up to mischief as usual," said Mr. Tibbs, wiping tears from his eyes. "Erasmus will have hidden him away somewhere to keep him from the corrupting influence of humans. I can assure you, there are absolutely *no* basilisks in St. Leonard's Forest."

"But what if there is one now?" I persisted.

"And what about the Dragonsbane ring?" added Beatrice. "Where could Erasmus have found it?"

"Oh, he could easily have borrowed it from his mother's hoard." Mr. Tibbs seemed to have an answer for everything. "Brythonnia had a very fierce reputation in the old days. I'm sure she has more than one Dragonsbane ring in her collection."

"But why would Erasmus play a prank at such an important time?" I cried. "Couldn't you at least tell Dr. Drake what has happened and let him decide — please?"

But Mr. Tibbs would not be swayed. "I think that Dr. Drake has enough on his plate at the moment, don't you?" he answered.

"I know, but, sir, Dr. Drake says that the threat from Dragonsbane must be taken seriously," Beatrice insisted. "I think he at least ought to know."

The jovial smile slipped from Mr. Tibbs face. "*I* will decide what Dr. Drake ought or ought not to know," he growled. "And I have had enough of your silly stories. Now, I have far more important matters to attend to. As for you children, you have two choices: either go and stay with Billy and Alicia Light — where you will be safe from Erasmus's infantile games — or go home and keep out of mischief."

"But what if Torcher doesn't come back?" Beatice asked helplessly.

"If you hear nothing from the chick in the next day or so," Mr. Tibbs said, sighing impatiently, "I suppose you had better return and let me know."

"Could Erasmus be playing games with us?" I asked Beatrice as we walked back along the corridor.

"I just don't see why he would," she answered. "If anything, I'd say he's too serious and puffed up with his own importance for jokes."

I grimaced. "One thing is plain, though. We *must* get a message to Dr. Drake."

"But how?" wailed Beatrice. "Mr. Tibbs won't help. And Mr. Flyte will just pass anything we tell him back to Mr. Tibbs."

"What about Billy and Alicia?" I brightened. "They could speak to their father."

"Yes, but we have no idea whether they will see their father or Dr. Drake any sooner than we will." Beatrice seemed to be losing hope.

"Then we must ask Erasmus whether he's been honest with us," I answered firmly.

By now we were passing Mr. Tibbs's office. On impulse I pushed the door open and looked inside.

"Daniel, what are you doing?" Beatrice demanded in a loud whisper.

"There's something about Mr. Tibbs that I just don't trust," I answered under my breath. "He's always against Dr. Drake. And he always comes up with excuses not to believe anything we say."

I stepped inside and was surprised by how small and cramped the office was. What struck me most, however, was that every surface in the room was covered with books and papers. It looked like a student's study on the night before an important examination. One large book on his desk caught my attention. It was entitled *The Handbook of Hoards—Dragon Treasure Through the Ages* by Archimedes Crook.

"*The Handbook of Hoards!*" I whispered. "What a wonderful title! Why have I never seen this book before?"

"Because, Daniel, some books at the S.A.S.D. are restricted to advanced dragonologists only," Beatrice scolded quietly.

"Then it looks as if Mr. Tibbs has been researching something."

I lifted the cover, and the book fell open on one of the pages Mr. Tibbs had marked. My eye was drawn to a detailed picture of the Dragon's Claw. Beneath it was a quotation:

"Diamond thwarts the action of certain poisons, prevents insanity, and banishes fear. Pliny the Elder."

"Look at this!" I said, forgetting to whisper in my excitement. "Wasn't Mr. Tibbs examining a replica of the Dragon's Claw?"

"*Shhh,* Daniel," warned Beatrice softly. "Perhaps you should shut the book before Mr. Tibbs comes back. He'll have us thrown out of the S.A.S.D. if he finds us going through his office. And we have to get that message to Dr. Drake."

"Listen to what it says here." This was too good to ignore, and I continued, lowering my voice a little.

"The diamond at the centre of the Dragon's Claw is the largest cut diamond in existence. It is many times larger than the famous Kohinoor Diamond and is of incalculable antiquity. It is priceless. Were they to become aware of its existence, kings and emperors would give away their kingdoms to own it.

"Can you believe it? I wonder who Archimedes Crook was."

"He was the Dragon Master before Ebenezer," Beatrice answered. "They must have been related."

As I started to close the book, I took note of the piece of paper that Mr. Tibbs had used to mark his place. It was, in fact, a newspaper clipping that bore the headline "Strange

Skeleton Unearthed at the Tower of London. The Missing Link between Birds and Reptiles?"

I had just started to read the article when Beatrice let out a loud gasp.

I turned towards her with my finger to my lips. She was pointing at a piece of paper on the wall. At the top of the sheet was the symbol of a *D*-rune, underneath which was written, *"Mort aux Dragons,"* then "The Oath of Allegiance to Dragonsbane," followed by a short speech in Latin.

"But I thought Mr. Tibbs didn't believe in Dragonsbane," I whispered.

"In which case," Beatrice replied, "why has he been researching them so thoroughly?"

She pointed to an ancient map on tattered brown paper that was pinned to the wall next to the Oath of Allegiance. It showed a labyrinth in which a maze of tunnels led to a central chamber. It was entitled, *"Les Catacombes des Dragons."*

"'The Dragon Catacombs'?" I gasped. "I wonder what they are."

"I don't know, but listen," said Beatrice urgently. "I think someone's coming."

Footsteps were advancing along the corridor. Seconds later, the door flew open, and in marched a furious Mr. Tibbs.

Chapter Seven
KIDNAPPED!

There is but one secret spot where a dragon may be slain
with certainty. Look under his scaly belly, and you shall
descry it: a soft, round spot a hands' breadth in
circumference. Strike there, and strike deep!
—— *Malleus Draconis, (The Hammer of the Dragons), Edvardus Rex*

Our journey home was slow, and as we gazed miserably from the carriage window, Mr. Tibbs's words resounded in my head: "So this was your plan, was it?" he had bellowed. "Spin me yarns about a missing dragon, try to distract me, then ransack my private papers!"

"Do you think Tibbs really meant it when he banned us from Dragonalia?" I ventured.

"Oh, he most certainly did," Beatrice replied. "Mr. Tibbs is often angry, but I have never seen him in quite such a fury."

"I thought he was going to explode." I giggled.

Beatrice gave a weak smile, but it quickly faded. "I am convinced Erasmus has not been lying to us," she murmured.

"But what can we do now?" I wailed. "How can we help Torcher?"

"We must send Erasmus to warn Dr. Drake about Tibbs at once!" Beatrice decided. "There is definitely something fishy going on."

We returned to the cottage that evening to find Darcy and Erasmus waiting for us by the ruined stable block.

"Is there any news?" asked Darcy anxiously. "Did you find Torcher?"

"No, we only found Mr. Tibbs. He was in a terrible fury and acting very suspiciously," I told him. "Especially after he found us going through his papers."

"No!" cried Darcy, smiling a little and shaking his head in disbelief.

Beatrice ignored him. "We need to get a message to Dr. Drake fast," she said. "Erasmus"—she turned to the Dragon's Apprentice with a serious expression on her face—"is there something that you are not telling us?"

The frost dragon looked puzzled. "I am not aware of any information that I am withholding from you," he protested huffily. "I circled London twice. There was no sign that Torcher or the basilisk had left the city."

"Mr. Tibbs suggested that you might be playing a trick on us," I explained.

"A trick?" Erasmus seemed horrified. "But why would

I do such a thing? Tricks are for children, not dragons. If it were a riddle, however, that would be another matter."

"Well, we don't have any time for riddles," I said sharply. "Now—"

But before I could say anything else, I heard the bell ring at the cottage door. It was unusual to have an unannounced guest, especially at this hour, and with our parents away from home.

"Do you think you've been followed?" asked Darcy.

"I didn't see anyone," replied Beatrice, thinking back to the rickety cart journey from the train to the cottage.

"I'll go, if you like," I offered, heading towards the back door of the cottage.

"But what about Erasmus?" Darcy asked.

"You wait here," I called behind me. "I shall whistle if it looks as though we need Erasmus to disappear."

I ran through the cottage and opened the front door, but, to my astonishment, there was no one there! I heard the sound of horses' hooves galloping along the track and looked about the garden for signs of a visitor. At last I spotted an envelope that had been left on the doorstep. It was addressed, *Daniel and Beatrice Cook*. I turned it over in my hands, and my blood ran cold, for the back of the envelope was embossed with the symbol of a *D*-rune.

I gulped and rushed straight back through the cottage to tell the others. "Whoever it was didn't wait." I panted, holding the envelope aloft and turning it over to reveal the symbol on the back. "They just left this."

Beatrice clapped a hand to her mouth. "Open it!" she cried.

With a pounding heart, I tore at the envelope, took out the parchment, and read,

"To Daniel and Beatrice Cook,

We have captured the young dragon Torcher, of whom we know you to be fond. But his torch will soon be put out unless you bring to us the treasure known as the Dragon's Claw. We have heard all about you, and we know that you can find this treasure for us. Tell no one if you want to see Torcher again.

Our agent will await you by the Eleanor Cross at Trafalgar Square at ten o'clock in the morning two days from now. He will wear a red feather in his lapel. Follow his instructions. Be warned, and be on time!

Mort aux Dragons! —D."

Beatrice covered her face with her hands "Poor Torcher— kidnapped by Dragonsbane!" she wailed. "I can hardly believe it."

"I knew they'd pull a dastardly stunt like this," said Darcy bitterly. "Protecting the lairs was never going to stop them."

"Well," I said, trying to look on the bright side, "at least we know who has him."

"But how can we ever get him back?" wailed Beatrice. "And how are we supposed to get the Dragon's Claw? We don't even know where it is."

"But we do know what it looks like." I imagined Tibbs holding the replica in his hand. "If we could just get hold of the replica, maybe we could use that instead."

"But Tibbs will never let us near it," Beatrice reminded me. I pictured the look of rage on Tibbs's face as we were leaving the shop and knew that she was right.

"But *I* know the whereabouts of the real Dragon's Claw," Erasmus announced unexpectedly. The three of us turned to look at him, desperate yet hopeful.

"Scramasax is its guardian," Erasmus continued.

"But she's Torcher's mother; we know her!" I exclaimed. "Surely she'll help us if her own chick is in danger." Scramasax had been too ill to attend the Dragon Rite two days earlier, because of the wounds she had received from Idraigir when Ignatius had enchanted him.

"She may be Torcher's mother," said Erasmus, "but I can promise you that, as a member of the Council of Dragons, she will never, ever surrender a treasure she has sworn to guard. Nor would she give in to vile blackmail, even if it meant risking the life of her own chick."

"Then we should get a message to Dr. Drake," urged Darcy. "He will know what to do."

"There's no need," Erasmus insisted as he examined his claws distractedly. "And, in any case, it would put Torcher's life in jeopardy. Surely this is a prime opportunity for revenge!" The young dragon lifted his head and gazed purposefully into the distance. "I shall fly to the Eleanor Cross with you, wherever that is, and smite their unmentionable agent! I will soon make him confess where they have hidden Torcher. Then I shall ensure that those hateful villains rue the day that ever a dragon was slain. I shall smash them with my tail and rip them with my claws. I shall breathe frost on them and turn them into icicles." I had never seen Erasmus so excited. He seemed so different from the dragon we had first encountered that I almost laughed out loud. Beatrice, however, did not share in my amusement.

"Erasmus!" she cried. "If you had not made Torcher run away in the first place, then none of this would have happened."

"That is why it is a matter of honour for me to set things straight," Erasmus replied with a show of humility I did not quite trust.

"Erasmus, you cannot travel to Trafalgar Square by day or by night," Beatrice reminded him. "Darcy is right; our only option is to tell Dr. Drake."

"Wait," I interrupted. "We all know there may be a traitor in the S.A.S.D. What if our message to Dr. Drake is intercepted? If that traitor finds out we've told anyone about the note, then Torcher will be—how did they say it?—'put out'!"

"Then perhaps we *should* find a way to give Dragons-bane the Dragon's Claw," mused Beatrice. "And, when Torcher is safe, we can find a way to get it back again."

"Give in to blackmail?" roared Erasmus, turning his head to one side and closing his eyes in disbelief. "Never!"

"What I don't understand is why Dragonsbane wants the Dragon's Claw in the first place," said Beatrice.

"It was one of their greatest weapons," replied Erasmus. "Fashioned for a Chinese ruler, called King Wu, over two thousand years ago. It was intended only to be used for good deeds. But since the day it was stolen — by one of Wu's own ministers — it has caused nothing but harm. You say you have seen the replica?"

"Oh, yes." I nodded enthusiastically.

"Good. Then you will know that it is the claw of a Chinese *lung* dragon holding a giant diamond." Erasmus explained that hundreds of years ago, the Claw had been awarded to the Earl of Norfolk as a prize for defeating a great Saracen knight in single combat. He had quickly spotted an opportunity to turn the great treasure into a powerful weapon.

The Earl had been an expert in the building of siege engines for warfare. One such weapon was the ballista, a kind of gigantic crossbow. In those days, few weapons could kill dragons but for one or two expertly made samurai swords, which could be obtained only in Japan and the Far East. Most ordinary weapons could not pass through a dragon's thick, scaly hide.

The Earl, however, believing the diamond to be the hardest of all natural substances, had tried an experiment. He had fitted the Dragon's Claw to the head of one of the quarrels on his ballista. On firing the weapon, he discovered it would penetrate almost any material—even dragon hide. Partly as a result of his discovery, the Earl had eventually become the first Master of Dragonsbane.

It had been Beatrice Croke, Erasmus continued, who had eventually taken the Dragon's Claw from Dragonsbane, having found it during a battle, thrust deep into the side of a dying dragon.

"Dragonsbane was defeated shortly afterwards, and they never saw the Claw again," Erasmus concluded.

"You know a great deal about the history of Dragonsbane," said Darcy, visibly impressed.

"And you know very little," Erasmus snapped back. "Fortunately, dragons do not commit their learning to books, where it may be lost or forgotten. They commit what they learn to their brains, where it can be remembered! And being the Dragon's Apprentice, I, of all dragons, should know about the history of the treasures that are so central to our pact, should I not?"

Erasmus gave us each a sharp look, then swiftly changed the subject. "What are you waiting for?" he demanded. "The dragon chick needs to be saved, does he not?"

"Erasmus is right," said Beatrice. "We must do something. Maybe we could speak to Scramasax."

"Certainly," agreed Erasmus. "I will take you."

"No, Erasmus," said Beatrice, who was obviously forming a plan in her head. "We must separate. You and Darcy go find Dr. Drake. Tell him everything that has happened; he will know what to do. But find a way to do it in secret. We don't want to give anything away to the traitor, whoever it may be."

"Shouldn't we all stick together?" I said, worried. "Surely it's safer that way."

"No," retorted Beatrice. "We've got too much to lose— Torcher's life is at stake! We'll have to travel to Scramasax's lair ourselves by train."

We had been to Ben Wyvis before and agreed that, until we heard from Dr. Drake, we should avoid any S.A.S.D. members who were guarding the path to the lair—and trust no one. We would then try to convince Scramasax to help Torcher.

"I can't think of another way," Beatrice said with a sigh. Neither one of us felt happy at the prospect of what lay ahead of us.

"I don't like it," I said. "But we have less than two days before the deadline! So you're right; we have to do something."

And so Darcy and Erasmus set off in search of Dr. Drake, whilst Beatrice and I picked up some of Father's dragonological field supplies and the money that Mother had left us to buy provisions. Within a few hours, we were speeding out of King's Cross Station under a starry sky on the overnight sleeper train to Edinburgh.

Chapter Eight

MR. ANDERSON

Among the dragon hoards are certain items of great value.
These you shall find described hereafter, and you must
render them unto the king. The rest, be they gold, silver,
or jewels aplenty, you may keep and dispose of as you wish.
—— *Malleus Draconis, (The Hammer of the Dragons), Edvardus Rex*

The train pulled in to Waverley Station at eight o'clock in the morning, and I was exhausted. I had not slept during the whole journey for worrying about Torcher. Beatrice looked in a similar state. We had just stood up to leave our compartment when a broad-shouldered man appeared in the doorway.

"Are you the Cook children? Beatrice and Daniel?" he asked pleasantly.

I nodded sleepily, and then remembered we had agreed to keep our mission a secret.

"Thank goodness I've found you." The man gave a sigh of relief and sat down on the edge of my bed. "Dr. Drake sent me. My name is Mr. Anderson."

I saw that his fist was held loosely at his side with one finger pointing towards the ground. It was the Sign of the Dragonological Apprentice. I made the same sign, and Mr. Anderson winked and smiled.

"When a dragon flies . . . ?" he whispered conspiratorially.

"He seeks it with his eyes," I said.

"Jolly good!" he exclaimed. "So you really are Beatrice and Daniel. One can never be too careful. I work for the Scottish division of the Society, and I am sorry to have to tell you that you are in great danger." He looked at us frankly. "People are following you."

"Are they from Dragonsbane?" I asked, rushing to the carriage window to see if I could catch a glimpse of them. "Where are they?" For some reason, I thought I might spot our pursuers in the crowds rushing about the station.

"Come away," hissed Mr. Anderson. "We are dealing with fanatical, dangerous men. It would be madness to confront them here. We must move quickly and give them the slip." He jumped up and stepped out of the carriage to check the corridor. "Have you any way of hiding your faces?" he asked.

"We could use our flameproof cloaks," I suggested, reaching into my pack.

"Good idea," Mr. Anderson replied. "Pull them right up over your heads." It was such a relief to have a sympathetic grown-up on our side. Beatrice and I covered our faces obediently and hurried after Mr. Anderson.

"Let us go along the corridor and alight at the end

nearest to the barrier," whispered Mr. Anderson. "That way we might escape notice."

We passed through the barrier without incident and ducked into a waiting room.

"Wait here," said Mr. Anderson. "I have to fetch something from the porter's office." He disappeared and returned a few moments later, dragging a heavy leather case behind him.

"What's that?" I asked.

"No need to worry about that," said Mr. Anderson. "Now, I saw the men who are following you on the platform. They seem angry. Where do we need to go next? Dr. Drake's telegram was brief. He just said to keep you safe from harm until he arrived and that you would explain everything to me once I found you."

"Have you heard any news of our parents?" I asked.

"I'm afraid not. But I'm sure we won't have to wait long for Dr. Drake to catch up with us — he will tell you all the latest news."

"But didn't he say what we should do?" asked Beatrice. "And why can't he come himself?" I was a little startled by my sister's brusqueness.

"Dr. Drake promised he would come as soon as he could, but at the moment he is involved in a very delicate and dangerous situation. Dragonsbane has turned out to be much more powerful than we thought. It seems they have been regrouping in secret for ages." Mr. Anderson looked grave. "He told me of your earlier adventures and assured me that you are both highly capable dragonologists. He seemed confident that you would follow the right course of action."

"We have to get to Ben Wyvis," I said. Beatrice shot me a fearsome glance, but I pretended not to notice. "We need to see Scramasax urgently."

"To Ben Wyvis?" exclaimed Mr. Anderson. "Then we must catch the next train to Inverness. Follow me—we don't have much time." He picked up his case, and we raced up onto a bridge and descended to another platform, slipping onto the Inverness train just as the conductor's whistle blew.

Mr. Anderson ushered us into a compartment and pulled down the blinds. He positioned himself next to the door, keeping a watchful eye out for our pursuers. As the train puffed its way through the valleys of the Grampian Mountains, I explained to him everything that had happened since Torcher had disappeared. Beatrice still seemed suspicious at first, but Mr. Anderson was so sympathetic, she soon lost her hostility.

"Those devils!" scoffed Mr. Anderson. "How could they stoop so low as to involve children in a conflict such as this! But rest assured, whoever these Dragonsbane types are, they will find that they have met their match with me! We shall find the Dragon's Claw *and* rescue Torcher, with or without Dr. Drake."

"But Scramasax won't let us have the Dragon's Claw," said Beatrice, her brow creased with worry. "According to Erasmus, dragons never give in to threats, whatever the cost."

"Don't concern yourself about that," Mr. Anderson said soothingly. "I'm sure that I can convince Scramasax to let us have the Dragon's Claw. We just need to approach her in the right way."

"Do you know Scramasax?" asked Beatrice, her face suddenly brightening with hope.

"No, sadly. Most of my work takes me farther west, out to the Hebrides. But where dragons are concerned, I do have a great deal of experience."

As the train pulled into Inverness Station, Mr. Anderson bade us stay in the carriage, whilst he unloaded his luggage and checked the train and platform for Dragonsbane men.

"All clear," he announced on his return, and he led us out to the station forecourt. "I have arranged our transportation." He smiled and stretched out an arm to indicate a neat little pony and trap. We hurried gratefully towards it, and I wondered how we should have managed had we been on our own.

"If we take the ferry across the Firth and go via Dingwall, then Ben Wyvis is about a twenty-mile journey from here."

"How long will that —?" I started to ask, but Beatrice had a more pressing question.

"What *have* you got in there?" she asked suspiciously, pointing to the leather case, which was tied onto the back of the trap. "Wouldn't it be quicker to leave it at the station?"

"It's dragonological equipment, if you must know," Mr. Anderson answered, waving a hand dismissively. "I thought it might come in handy."

"What sort of equipment?" I asked, eyeing the case with interest.

"Just a few special items that have proved useful in the past," Mr. Anderson replied.

"Such as . . . ?" Beatrice asked.

"My, you are a curious pair." He laughed. "Well, Dr. Drake did warn me of that. I promise you'll find out the contents if there's any cause to use them. But for now, time is pressing, and we have a dragon chick to rescue!"

Mr. Anderson hopped onto the front of the cart, and once Beatrice and I were seated in the back, he cracked a whip, and the pony set off at a startling pace. We soon reached the road, which was relatively smooth, but as it turned onto a dirt track, Beatrice and I had to hold on tight for fear we might be flung from the cart. We took the cart across on the ferry without incident, passed through Dingwall, and began heading into the mountains at a more stately pace.

I noticed that Mr. Anderson kept casting glances back over his shoulder.

"Do you really think they are following us?" I shouted. It was hard to converse over the noise of the cart as it rumbled along the bumpy track.

"I'm certain that someone followed you as far as Edinburgh," he called back. "They must have kept watch on your cottage after they had delivered their note. But we seem to have evaded them for now."

"Why would they follow us?" Beatrice queried.

"If they can take the Dragon's Claw from you before you have a chance to exchange it," Mr. Anderson explained, "then they won't need to spare Torcher's life, will they? And they might manage to put an end to Scramasax, too."

I suddenly felt rather sick, both from the discomfort of the journey and at the thought that we could have led Dragonsbane straight to Scramasax's lair.

The cart drew to a halt at last; we had reached the foot of the mountain. Mr. Anderson turned to us. "We shall have to walk from here," he told us. "But we need to be on the lookout in case there is an S.A.S.D. volunteer guarding the route to Scramasax's lair."

"Couldn't we ask them to help us?" Beatrice suggested.

Mr. Anderson looked horrified. "We must avoid them at all costs! If, as you suspect, there is a traitor in the S.A.S.D., we shall have to be extremely careful whom we trust." He turned and began scanning the mountainside. "Now, which way is the lair?"

"The tunnel entrance lies on the other side of the mountain," I told him.

Mr. Anderson tied up the pony and ran a little way along the various tracks on the mountainside. "Let us take a route that avoids the main path," he suggested as he ran back to hoist the mysterious case from the back of the cart.

"Are you sure you are going to need all that equipment?" asked Beatrice. It would certainly slow us down.

"Possibly not, but I cannot leave it here for just anyone

to find," Mr. Anderson answered. "Besides, it may come in useful. So, Daniel, if you don't mind, could you help me carry it?"

I took one end of the long case. Between us, we could just about manage it. The case swung as we carried it, making the equipment inside clang and rattle as we went. We edged slowly round the mountain, the case growing heavier with every step. I wondered what kind of equipment could possibly be worth so much effort.

At last I caught a whiff of a familiar sulphurous odour. Farther along the track lay a scattered trail of deer and sheep bones that had been picked clean: we were close to the lair at last.

We hid behind a rocky outcrop for a short while, to avoid coming into contact with anyone from the S.A.S.D.

"There doesn't seem to be anyone here," Beatrice whispered after a while.

"Nor is there any sign of Dr. Drake," said Mr. Anderson, looking about for any movement. "I think we will need to speak to Scramasax ourselves."

We walked a little farther, cautiously drawing closer to the lair.

"What is your plan?" asked Mr. Anderson under his breath. He began lowering his end of the case, and, with relief, I did likewise. We peered curiously into the dark, craggy cave entrance.

"Unless you have a better idea, we planned simply to go

in and talk to Scramasax," I explained. "But it's going to be difficult. She has a terrible temper, and we have it on good authority that she won't give in to blackmail—even to save her chick."

"And if we aren't very careful, she'll fly straight to London to search for him," Beatrice added. Then, addressing Mr. Anderson, she asked, "How do you think we can convince her to let us have the Dragon's Claw?"

"I think it will be best done out here on the mountainside," replied Mr. Anderson. "Dragons do not like unknown people to enter their lairs, do they? As you have met this dragon before and I have only ever seen her from a distance, I suggest you two go in and invite her to come outside and speak to me. Let her know that Dr. Drake is on his way; that may help to soften her mood. Once she's outside, I will convince her to surrender her treasure."

Mr. Anderson's plan sounded sensible, and we readily agreed to it. I lit a candle, and Beatrice and I hurried in through the tunnel entrance. Inside, the lair was pleasantly warm, though the sulphurous smell grew stronger and more abhorrent as we progressed deeper into the rock. Gradually the light dimmed, and we could hear nothing at first but the echoing drips of rainwater that had penetrated the cave walls.

We passed the skull and crossbones that had been arranged on the floor to deter intruders and noticed a message written in runes on the wall. I remembered that we had not been able to decipher it the last time we had visited Scramasax's lair. This time, I held the candle close and Beatrice read out, "'Here be dragons.'" We exchanged an excited but apprehensive look.

"Do you think Scorcher will remember us?" I asked her.

"I'm sure he will." She smiled at the thought of seeing Torcher's older brother again.

A moment later, there came a scrabbling, fluttering sound. A creature was half running, half flying towards us. It did not stop as it reached us, and Beatrice and I were soon knocked right off our feet. Hot, sulphurous dragon breath assaulted our nostrils, and a rough, leathery tongue swept across both our faces. Scorcher had not forgotten us.

"*Praisich hoyari!*" he roared.

"Scorcher, stop!" exclaimed Beatrice, giggling as she picked herself up. "*Praisich boyar!* But you have to be more gentle with guests," she scolded kindly. "Yes, we've come to visit you, but we also need to speak to your mother. Is she here?"

Scorcher trotted off ahead of us, holding his head on one side to keep us in view. I thought back to the last time we had visited the lair. It was just before Torcher was born. Inside, the heat had been unbearable as, every few hours, Scramasax had blown a jet of white-hot flame across her egg. As if the heat did not cause us enough discomfort, we were also in the company of Ignatius Crook at the time. I shuddered at the memory.

Scorcher led us into the central chamber and waited close to the entrance. The chamber walls glittered with dragon dust. I gasped at the brilliance of the huge mound of treasure. It filled the room. Even in the dim light of my candle, gold and silver glistened and gem-encrusted trinkets sparkled. I studied the hoard carefully, hopeful that I might spot the Dragon's Claw, but I did not.

It took a moment before I spotted Scramasax, slumped atop the glistening treasure hoard. She was breathing heavily and did not look well. Raising her head slowly, she sniffed the air.

"Daniel and Beatrice Cook!" she said, her yellow eyes focusing keenly upon us. "My young friends. To me it seems hardly a day since you were last here, yet it is more than a year, is it not?"

"We bring news that cannot wait," explained Beatrice. "But first we must enquire after your health. Are you recovered from your wounds?"

Scramasax slowly shook her crested head. The question was answered before she spoke. "Idraigir's fangs sank deep into my flesh," Scramasax began. It sounded as though even speech was an effort for her. "Such wounds take more than one year to heal, but as I rest, I begin to feel a little restored. Scorcher is helping, as you see." We turned towards the dragon chick, and he seemed to beam with pride.

"How is his little brother?" Scramasax enquired. "I hear that you have given him the name Torcher!"

"You can be very proud of him," I told her. "He represented you with honour at the Dragon Rite."

"Yes, so I heard." Scramasax nodded graciously. "You have trained him well."

Scramasax shifted slightly on top of her hoard, sending

golden chains, silver cups, and priceless jewels skittering to the floor. "These are troubled times, however," she continued. "They say that the dragon slayers have returned. Do you know this to be true?"

"Alas, it is so." I bowed my head, ashamed of the news I had to share with her. "This is, in fact, why we have come. I am sorry to have to tell you that Torcher has been kidnapped by Dragonsbane."

"What?" cried Scramasax, raising her head suddenly.

"Beatrice and I received a message," I went on. "It says that they will return Torcher only in exchange for——" But before I could complete the sentence, Scramasax let out a roar of rage and anguish so loud that the ground shook beneath our feet, the treasure hoard rattled, and more trinkets tumbled to the floor. Covering my ears was no protection from the ear-splitting wails that followed.

Black smoke billowed from Scramasax's nostrils, and she flicked her tail violently. "Where are these vile men who have taken my Torcher?" she raged. "Sick as I am, I will burn them, claw them into a thousand smithereens! They shall not survive my wrath! What is it that they would dare to barter for the return of my chick?"

"The Dragon's Claw," replied Beatrice a little timidly. Although Scramasax did not direct her wrath at us, her anger was ferocious; few would not have been intimidated.

"The Dragon's Claw?" she snarled. "Even if I had it, I would never give it to them!"

"What do you mean? *Don't* you have the Claw?" Beatrice was astounded.

"But Erasmus told us that you were its guardian," I exclaimed, confused.

"And so I am, but I am sick. In these dangerous times, Idraigir has taken it. The S.A.S.D. did not have sufficient volunteers to give protection to my lair, so the Dragon's Claw has been taken for safekeeping. You must visit Idraigir at Wharncliffe to retrieve it." I groaned with frustration; we had wasted so much time. "But tell me, quickly," Scramasax implored, "how all this came to pass."

Beatrice and I hurriedly explained everything that had happened over the last few days. The dragon listened thoughtfully, her brow furrowed with worry, her eyes narrow and watery.

"Are you sure that Erasmus went to speak to Dr. Drake?" she asked at last. "You must know how much he dislikes humans."

"We believe the frost dragon's intentions were to do as we had asked him. He feels responsible for Torcher's fate," Beatrice told her. "But Darcy also went with him."

"Hmm." Scramasax seemed to approve. "I have heard good things of this Darcy. But I am surprised he is not with you! I know you are not alone; there is the scent of another human in the air. Who is it? Have you left him outside my lair?"

"It's Mr. Anderson," I explained hurriedly, aware that we would need to move fast if we were to get to Idraigir in time to retrieve the Dragon's Claw and save Torcher. "He is a member of the Secret and Ancient Society. Dr. Drake sent him to help us, and he wishes to talk to you."

"He believes that he will convince me to let you have the Dragon's Claw, does he not?" Scramasax declared. "Are you sure that he is all that he seems?"

"Of course," I said. "We were was suspicious of him at first, but he's been so kind and helpful."

"Then let us go and meet this Mr. Anderson," said Scramasax. Slowly she began to uncoil her scaly body and slither down from the top of her hoard, pieces of treasure clattering to the floor as she moved.

"Scorcher, stand guard!" she ordered, and the little dragon straightened as if at attention. She began edging her way towards the tunnel. We walked slowly, a few steps ahead of her.

"Now, who is this Mr. Anderson?" she seemed to be addressing the question to herself. "I think it is time to find out."

CHAPTER NINE

THE BATTLE OF BEN WYVIS

Knights, go forth and slay these scaly beasts with joy in your
hearts and a song upon your lips! Slay them gladly, looking
forward to the day when you can in all honesty say to your
children: there is no such thing as a dragon!

— *Malleus Draconis (The Hammer of the Dragons), Edvardus Rex*

The sudden return to daylight blinded me for a moment,
and at first I could not see Mr. Anderson. Then I spotted him. He was kneeling about thirty feet away, behind
the muzzle of what I can only describe as a small cannon. I
could feel my heart sinking.

"Beatrice, stay back. He's got a gun!" I shouted.

"You are a perceptive boy, Daniel," sneered Mr. Anderson.
"It *is* a gun: a portable field gun, in fact. It packs quite a
punch, as you will see. Now, don't try anything stupid, either
of you. I don't want to hurt you unless I really have to."

"How could I have been so stupid?" I cried. "He's part of
Dragonsbane!"

"You can't shoot dragons with guns!" Beatrice shouted to him defiantly. She had never been as sure of Mr. Anderson as I had, and I was slowly realising that the situation we found ourselves in was all due to my own stupidity.

"Move aside," Anderson snarled. "You won't get another chance. I just want Scramasax and the Dragon's Claw."

"When Scramasax sees you with that, she will kill you before you get a chance to use it!" I yelled with real hatred in my voice. I marvelled at the thought that I had believed all the lies Anderson had told us.

There came a sudden rumbling from inside the tunnel as Scramasax made her way towards the entrance.

"Scramasax, look out!" I yelled. Mr. Anderson had already leapt into action. With a blinding flash and a sharp retort, a thunderous explosion shook the mountainside above me. I scrambled out of the way, dragging Beatrice with me as a shower of small rocks and dirt pelted us from above. Mr. Anderson had blasted a hole measuring roughly ten feet across in the solid granite of the ben. Below us, a small rocky avalanche tumbled down the mountainside.

"That's just a taste," Mr. Anderson said with a leer as he reloaded. "Now that you know what it can do, you'd better get out of the way!"

An angry roar bellowed from the tunnel behind me. I struggled to my feet, desperate to do something to stop all this. A furious Scramasax burst from the tunnel mouth and thundered towards Anderson, flames of orange fire gushing from her mouth. Anderson remained completely calm. He merely sighted along the barrel of his gun and pulled the trigger once more. I couldn't breathe for fear of what might happen next, but I struggled to try to get closer to Anderson. Another explosion sent yet more broken rock tumbling to the valley floor and knocked Scramasax right off her feet. But Mr. Anderson had missed. I breathed again.

Scramasax let out another furious roar. I felt sure that once she was back on her feet, she would move swiftly, reaching Mr. Anderson before he had a chance to reload for a second time. Scramasax was still weak from her wounds, however, and Mr. Anderson had already loaded another explosive shell.

Luckily, I had by this time managed to get around to Mr. Anderson's side, knowing that he couldn't focus on two targets at once. Beatrice was right behind me. Scramasax leapt at Mr. Anderson, who brought his gun up to aim point-blank at her underbelly. He could not miss. But just before he pulled the trigger, Beatrice and I threw ourselves at the barrel of the gun, pushing it away just before the third explosion. Now Scramasax could reach to swipe at Mr. Anderson with her tail. He flew high into the air and landed a good fifteen feet away, his leg bent awkwardly beneath him. Scramasax lunged towards him and opened her jaws wide.

"Stop, Scramasax!" cried Beatrice, rushing to push herself between the dragon and Mr. Anderson. "Stop! Don't kill him!"

"I *will* kill him!" roared Scramasax, raising a claw to strike.

"No!" I cried. "You mustn't."

"Why not?" cried Scramasax. "This man is a thief. *He* wants to kill *you,* does he not? He does not deserve your protection! I will take that stupid metal thing, and I will crush it into a thousand pieces. And then I will incinerate the man who dares to barter with me over the treasure I guard and my own precious chick. I will gnaw on his scorched bones. I will—"

"No, please," cried Beatrice desperately. "Remember the pact!"

"Beatrice is right," I joined in. "To kill a human now, or for any human to kill a dragon, would sour relations between humans and dragons forever."

Mr. Anderson scrambled to his feet and tried to run, but his injured leg would not let him; he slipped and fell to the ground. Scramasax roared again. But it was only now that I could see how exhausted the short fight had made her. She had certainly not yet recovered her strength.

"He knows where my chick is!" the weary dragon wailed. "Let me at least make him tell!"

"She's right." Beatrice turned to me. "We *do* need to know where Torcher is."

Scramasax lowered her head towards Mr. Anderson. He was leaning on his good knee now, white as a sheet and shaking like a leaf. His machine lay on its side next to the open case and a few cartridges that had spilled out from it.

"Tell me," she said as she pressed her scaly muzzle closer

to his face. "Where is my son?" Her voice was low, but its tone was menacing; her hot breath turned Anderson's white face red. Beads of sweat pricked his forehead. He could barely speak.

"In th-th-ere," he stammered, pointing his shaking hand towards the empty case that had held his precious machine. "L-l-look in there."

As we turned to follow the direction of his finger, Mr. Anderson began limping down the mountain as fast as he could.

Scramasax sat down with a thud. I approached the gun case cautiously and took a look inside. It didn't seem to contain much to get excited about, just a few tools and a portfolio of papers. When I unfurled the papers, however, I gasped. I held in my hands the exact same map of the Dragon Catacombs that we had seen in Mr. Tibbs's office in London.

"How did Anderson get his hands on this?" I marvelled, turning to show Beatrice what I had found.

Her eyes widened as she studied the parchment carefully. "It is the same in every detail." She grimaced. "Mr. Tibbs is a despicable beast!"

"Surely he can't have anything to do with this?" I was openmouthed at the suggestion. Mr. Tibbs worked for the government. He was involved at the very heart of the S.A.S.D.

"Isn't it obvious?" sniffed Beatrice. "Mr. Tibbs has taken us all for a ride! Why else would he keep pooh-poohing the whole idea of Dragonsbane, whilst secretly researching it?

He's been a part of this dreadful scheme from the very start! Think about it." Beatrice was almost as furious as Scramasax. "Mr. Tibbs could easily have revealed the locations of the dragons' lairs to Dragonsbane."

"But what possible reason could he have to want to cause dragons any harm?" I asked. Despite Mr. Tibbs's hot temper and his hostility towards Dr. Drake, it was hard to think of a motive for his betrayal of the society.

"I have no idea," Beatrice answered. "But this would explain why he always goes against Dr. Drake. Remember how uncomfortable he seemed at the Dragonological Dinner when Lord Chiddingfold suggested there might be a traitor in the S.A.S.D. ranks?" Beatrice put her hands on her hips. "*He* was the traitor!"

At last I could see that Beatrice might be onto something. I clicked my fingers. "Then he must also know where Torcher is!" I declared.

"Of course," Beatrice answered. "But let's hope there is also some sort of clue on the parchment."

I had almost forgotten that I had the map in my hand. I turned back to study it more closely. There was handwriting scribbled all over it and a small note tacked to one corner, written in a different hand.

"I'm sure the map we saw wasn't covered in scribbles," I said. "But otherwise it is just the same, isn't it?"

"Oh, quite definitely," Beatrice agreed. "Someone must

have added to it since we last saw Tibbs. What does the writing say?"

"I don't know." I studied the words more carefully, but it was no use; they were complete gobbledegook to me. "I think it's all in French."

Beatrice snatched the parchment from my hand. "Listen to this!" she exclaimed. "The note attached to the map says, '*L'entrée se situe à la base de la Tour de Lanthorn.*' 'The entrance is situated in the base of the Lanthorn Tower'!"

"Where's that?" I asked.

Beatrice shrugged. "I have no idea," she replied.

"Do you think they're hiding Torcher there?" I could hardly bear to think of our poor little chick imprisoned underground. I wondered about his companion. "Does it say anything about a basilisk?" I queried.

"There's nothing else on the note, but let me check the map." Beatrice was silent for a few moments, then at last she said, "The handwriting seems to be some sort of instruction. It says, '*Appuyez sur les yeux et tirez la langue.*' 'Press the eyes and pull the tongue'? It doesn't make any sense."

I noticed some letters on the map itself, and there seemed to be a key down one side. I pointed it out. "Can you decipher this?" I asked.

Next to the letter *A* on the key was a picture of three dragon heads, identical but for the colour of their eyes. One had a red eye, one green, and the other blue. Underneath was written the words, *"Pour arrêter les larmes d'acide, fermez l'oeil rouge."*

"'To stop the tears of acid, close the red eye,'" Beatrice translated.

"I do wish it wasn't all in French," I cried in frustration.

"But that was the main language of the Dragonsbane Knights," explained Scramasax, looking over Beatrice's shoulder.

"How stupid," I scoffed. "Speaking in French when they were all English!"

"Actually, the French language came to our shores with the king you call William the Conqueror. It was only at the time of King Edward Longshanks that the English language began to become more popular."

"This is remarkable!" Beatrice interrupted, ignoring Scramasax's history lesson. "Right in the centre of the maze here," she pointed, "it says, *'Utilisez la Serre du Dragon ici.'* 'Use the Dragon's Claw here'!"

I didn't have a chance to reply.

"Look to the west," Scramasax cried suddenly. "Dr. Drake is coming. He is flying with Idraigir and Erasmus!"

"Oh, thank goodness!" said Beatrice, though we could see nothing. Scramasax's eyesight was far better than ours or that of any human. Little by little, however, the shapes of two flying dragons became visible, and a few minutes later, Idraigir and Erasmus had landed on the mountainside. The dragons waited a short distance away, whilst Dr. Drake ran across to us.

"My dears! Are you all right?" he shouted as he approached. "I'm so sorry that I could not come more quickly," he continued. "There was an attack on Tregeagle. Your parents were brave, but they would not have held off the enemy without aid. The battle was still raging when Erasmus arrived."

"Are our parents all right?" asked Beatrice anxiously.

"Don't worry, my dears. They are both fine," Dr. Drake assured her. "One or two of the attackers ended up a lot colder than they would have liked." He chuckled, glancing across at Erasmus, but the smile slipped from Dr. Drake's face when he caught sight of the field gun.

"What's this doing here?" he asked.

"Mr. Anderson brought it with him," I said. "It's already blown up a large part of the mountain."

"Who on earth is Mr. Anderson?" asked Dr. Drake, looking incredulously from the two of us to the gun and back again.

"He's a member of Dragonsbane," Beatrice explained. "He met us on the train at Edinburgh. He told us that you had sent him."

"Did he indeed!" The mild-tempered Dr. Drake seemed suddenly rather agitated.

"He knew the secret signs and passwords and everything," I added, knowing full well that we should have been more suspicious of him.

Dr. Drake mopped his brow and pulled at his moustache as he surveyed the damage around the entrance to

Scramasax's lair. "If Dragonsbane has weapons that can do such damage to solid granite, one wonders what need they have for the ancient treasures." He turned his piercing gaze upon us. "And where is Mr. Anderson now?" he asked.

"He cannot be far away," I answered. "He has a badly injured leg."

Dr. Drake turned to stride back towards the mighty dragon. "Then Idraigir and I will find him at once before he gets up to any more mischief," he called.

"Wait," I cried. Dr. Drake stopped in his tracks and turned to face me. "Mr. Anderson *did* do us a service. He helped us to uncover the traitor."

"The traitor?" Dr. Drake seemed surprised. "And who might that be?"

"It's Mr. Tibbs!" Beatrice answered, holding out the map.

"Oh, come, come now." Dr. Drake laughed. "Is this some sort of joke?" He took the map from Beatrice, then gave a start. "Where on earth did you get this? A map of the Catacombs of Dragonsbane . . ."

He stared at the map in wonderment, with Idraigir peering curiously over his shoulder.

"It's from Mr. Tibbs!" I burst out. "He gave it to Mr. Anderson. When we went to see him after Torcher had been kidnapped, we found him in the room with the replicas of the twelve treasures. He was studying the Dragon's Claw — the exact treasure the kidnappers are after. He denied that

Dragonsbane existed, but when we looked in his office afterwards, it was full of things relating to them."

"You looked in his office?" Dr. Drake glared at us. He was not impressed.

"We didn't trust him," I tried to explain.

"When we told him that Torcher had disappeared, he refused to pass the message on to you," Beatrice added.

"So we thought we ought to check up on him," I continued, nervous of the expression on Dr. Drake's face, "and, lo and behold, we found this map in his office, and a copy of the Dragonsbane Oath!"

Dr. Drake's brow creased in concern as he looked from me to Beatrice. "I don't know quite what to say," he said. "This is all rather difficult to take in. Mr. Tibbs has been a loyal member of the S.A.S.D. for many years—I don't understand how he could have—"

"There is a note with the map," Beatrice interjected, handing it to him. "It says that the entrance to the Dragon Catacombs can be found at the base of the Lanthorn Tower, wherever that is."

"The base of the Lanthorn Tower?" Dr. Drake repeated. "At least that explains something."

"Explains what?" I asked.

"The Lanthorn Tower is at the Tower of London. It burned down a hundred years ago and was left as a ruin for some time, but it's currently being restored."

"So, the entrance to the catacombs is at the Tower of London!" I exclaimed.

"And the renovations have allowed Dragonsbane to gain access to it again," Beatrice observed. "That must be where they are keeping Torcher."

"And it's also why Mr. Tibbs wants the Dragon's Claw," I stated with some satisfaction. "It's marked on the map; look. 'Use the Dragon's Claw here.'" It all fell into place. Dr. Drake had to agree with us: Tibbs was looking very guilty indeed.

"Well, the two of you have done very well, as usual." Dr. Drake nodded slowly. "I shall certainly get to the bottom of this, though I still find it very difficult to believe that Tibbs has anything to do with this business. Idraigir and I can take over from here," Dr. Drake continued. "We will find Mr. Anderson—or whatever his real name is—and then we shall see about getting the Dragon's Claw and rescuing Torcher."

"What about us?" asked Beatrice, a little crestfallen that we were no longer to pursue the Dragon's Claw.

"Well, we need to get you somewhere safe." Dr. Drake scratched his head for a moment. "I suggest you head for Lord Chiddingfold's house in London. The address is Twenty-two St. James's Square. Warn him that Mr. Tibbs *may* not be all that he seems—though I will need to see more hard evidence before I condemn him, mind you. Tell him I am on my way, and that, until I arrive, he should do nothing except keep a careful eye on Tibbs."

I felt a wave of exhaustion sweep over me after all we

had been through over the last couple days. "It will take us hours to get back to London by train," I complained.

"Then Erasmus will take you," said Idraigir, looking for agreement from the frost dragon and finding none. "Won't you, Erasmus?" he insisted.

"What?" Erasmus looked anything but pleased. "I do not know if I can carry two children *that* far. I am still tired after flying that fat Darcy boy."

"A dragon's life is in danger, "snapped Idraigir. "And whilst you are my apprentice and I am Guardian, you will do as I ask. You still have much to learn about conserving and protecting humans!"

"Very well." Erasmus sighed. "Climb on, children, though I cannot promise you a comfortable ride."

"You will make it as comfortable as possible," ordered Idraigir, finally losing his patience with the moody young dragon. "And then you will report straight back to me!"

Erasmus held his head high but kept silent as we climbed onto his back. With a few quick steps and a steady flapping of his wings, he took off, and we were on our way.

"Farewell, Scramasax!" I called. "May your wounds heal quickly!"

"Farewell, my young friends," Scramasax replied. "We shall meet again soon. I am certain of it." I watched the great dragon making her way slowly towards her lair, growing smaller and smaller as we rose up into the clouds.

Beatrice and I clung on tightly as we flew over the tops

of the Grampian Mountains. Presently Erasmus softened a little and asked for news of all that had happened since we had last seen him. We gladly obliged, though after a while our voices became hoarse from shouting loud enough for him to hear us.

"It seems the information I gave you regarding the Dragon's Claw was out of date," Erasmus called back to us rather stiffly. "I am sorry if that put you in unnecessary danger."

Beatrice and I exchanged a look. An apology from Erasmus! This was most unexpected.

"We can stop at Wharncliffe and fetch the Claw, if you would like," he offered. "My mother, Brythonnia, is guarding the cave. She has been staying there since her attack, keeping watch in the Guardian's Chamber, whilst Idraigir and Dr. Drake have been directing the defence against Dragonsbane."

Beatrice was doubtful. "Do you really think Brythonnia would give the Claw to us?"

"Perhaps not," Erasmus replied. "In that case, I shall leave that task to Dr. Drake and Idraigir and do my best to fly you straight to London." He suddenly beat his wings furiously and rose higher into the sky. We could feel the air cooling around us and huddled next to his scaly body for warmth. "Hold on tight," the dragon cried. "I am going to fly you more swiftly than you have ever been flown before."

CHAPTER TEN

LONDON

Touch not the dragon, but a glove!

—— *Malleus Draconis (The Hammer of the Dragons), Edvardus Rex*

E rasmus grumbled from time to time, but he showed no sign of tiring as he flew south. The ride was swift, but it was also very bumpy. As the sun began to set and the sky grew dark, the frost dragon turned his head to speak.

"It will not be long before we reach London," he cried, much to our relief. "Since we are arriving at nighttime, I shall set you down in one of the parks. I do not think that I will be seen."

"You could try Hyde Park," I suggested. I knew there was enough open space there for Erasmus to land easily, and I had a feeling Lord Chiddingfold's house was not far from there. "It should be easy to spot from the air, because of the boating lake. What do they call it?" I turned to Beatrice.

"You mean the Serpentine," she answered immediately, as I knew she would.

"Then Hyde Park is our destination," Erasmus confirmed. "And then what will you do?" He seemed genuinely concerned.

"Beatrice and I will try to find Lord Chiddingfold and get help. If Mr. Tibbs keeps to the two days mentioned in the ransom note, then we have only a matter of hours to find out where he is hiding Torcher. I just hope Dr. Drake and Idraigir can get to us in time."

"I shall find Idraigir and tell him you are safe."

"But first," I begged, "do you think you could fly to Dragonsbrook and let Darcy know what has happened?"

"And warn him about Mr. Tibbs?" Beatrice added.

Erasmus nodded his snow-white head.

The air was clear and growing colder as night approached, but at least it didn't rain. Lights twinkled in the towns below us and all along the Great North Road. Though he flew high up in the sky, Erasmus followed the road, knowing it would eventually lead us to London.

At last a broad pool of gaslights stretching for miles in every direction told us that we had arrived in the big city. We smiled with relief and in wonder at the sight of the capital at night. Erasmus flew on towards the centre, and as the streets broadened, we kept a lookout for open parkland.

"Over there," Beatrice cried, pointing suddenly. "Could that be Hyde Park?"

"Erasmus," I cried, "the Serpentine lake is shaped like a fat snake. Can you see anything like that?"

"There *is* a lake," Erasmus confirmed. "But it is not in the shape of a serpent. It looks more like an arrowhead from this direction. I see cages with lions. There is an elephant, too, and some sort of white bear."

"It's a polar bear!" Beatrice laughed, happy that we could at least identify our location. "That must be Regent's Park. The animals belong to London Zoo!"

We could not be far from Hyde Park. I had seen plenty of maps of London. I closed my eyes and tried to visualize one in my head.

"We need to fly a little bit farther southwest," I said, thinking hard. "Can you see a park in that direction?"

"There is a rectangular park with two lakes," said Erasmus. "One of them looks like a snake as it bends around to the left."

"That must be the Serpentine!" I shouted eagerly. I opened my eyes again. "Can you land there?"

Erasmus stayed high in the sky until the very last moment, when he hovered over the a large square of rich green grass and then quickly swooped in low, his large claws ready to touch down. But just as he was about to land, we heard two startled screams—one from a man, the other from a woman. Erasmus was swiftly airborne again.

"Where else we can land near here?" asked Beatrice.

"There's Green Park," I suggested, consulting the map

in my head. I called to Erasmus. "Can you see another park, just beyond this one?"

Erasmus nodded and began swooping down towards a large expanse of lawn. He landed with a gentle thud.

It was such a relief to be on the ground at last. Beatrice and I dismounted. There was no one in sight, but Erasmus turned quickly to leave, eager that no one should catch sight of him. "Good luck," he whispered as he prepared to take off.

I was startled. "Careful, Erasmus!" I said with a laugh. "You are wishing humans luck. You wouldn't be changing your mind about us, would you?"

The frost dragon gave me an irritated look. "Go with dragon speed!" he hissed. "And find out what has happened to that little chick."

We needed to move fast. We did not stop to watch Erasmus fly off into the night. Nor did we stop to wonder at the strange habits of the flamingos that stood around the edge of a small lake. They slept upright, and on one leg!

"Beatrice," I hissed, "I don't think Green Park has a lake."

"Doesn't it?" She threw me a startled look.

"I've never heard of one with a flock of flamingos, either," I whispered.

"Well, I'm no expert on London's green spaces," she replied. "But you seem to know quite a bit about them. Where do *you* think we have landed?"

Across the park was an enormous building that seemed somehow familiar. It was three or four storeys high, with classical pillars, long rectangular windows, and carved panels along the walls. There was even a flag flying from the roof.

"Oh, no!" I gasped, realising with horror where we were. "Erasmus has left us in the middle of Buckingham Palace Gardens!"

"What?" exclaimed Beatrice. "Then we'd better get out of them, and quickly!"

We passed the lake and began skirting the edge of the gardens only to meet with an impossibly high wall topped with nasty-looking iron spikes.

"Perhaps one of the side gates will be open," suggested Beatrice.

"It's worth a try," I agreed. We were heading back along the edge of the wall towards the palace when, all at once, we heard furious barking.

"Dogs!" exclaimed Beatrice, and she froze to the spot.

"Doesn't the queen keep some as pets?" I asked, desperately trying to think of a way to reassure my sister.

"Yes, but those are only little Pomeranians," Beatrice wailed. "These sound more like great big German shepherds!"

I didn't like to think what would happen should the dogs be let off their leads to sniff us out. They would certainly smell dragon scent on our clothes, and I had no idea how they would react. "There's nothing else to do," I admitted hopelessly. "We'll have to look for a guard and ask him to take us to Lord Chiddingfold." Reluctantly we turned and started walking back towards the palace buildings.

Soon the barking was amplified with shouts. Lights flashed on at a side entrance to the palace, and upstairs on the second floor, a window opened.

We held our hands above our heads, and I cried out, "We surrender! We mean no harm."

"We're children!" shouted Beatrice, her voice a little wobbly. "We'll come quietly."

Moments later, three men began marching across the lawn towards us, lanterns swinging at their sides. I guessed they must be from the queen's foot guards. Two were dressed in red uniforms with bearskin hats and long rifles. The third wore a black police constable's uniform. They each held a leash at which a dog strained angrily. Beatrice had been right; they really did look savage.

Something made me glance towards the upstairs window. A figure leaned out of it, but I caught only a glimpse before it vanished inside again and the window closed.

"Stay where you are!" the policemen ordered. "Keep your hands where I can see them!"

The three men marched up to where we were standing, their dogs salivating as they advanced.

"I'm terribly sorry—" Beatrice began, but the men acted as though she hadn't said a word.

"Well, well," said the first foot guard, letting his snarling dog sniff at our knees. "They don't have the appearance of your regular urchins. They're too well dressed for that."

"How did you two get in here?" the second foot guard

demanded. "I've been on guard all night, and I didn't see you."

"Well—" I started to explain.

"You must have been dozing, then, mustn't you?" said the first foot guard, answering his colleague's question but completely ignoring Beatrice and me. His dog was becoming agitated. Had it smelled the dragon scent?

"What shall we do with them?" asked the policeman.

"It's too late to question them now," the second foot guard replied, pulling his dog away from us to stand behind him. "We'll lock them up in the guardhouse tonight. Your police people can deal with them tomorrow."

He wagged a finger at us menacingly. I felt furious that we were being treated like common criminals, but, more important, I was worried about Torcher. We couldn't waste another night. There was only one day left to find him before Dragonsbane would carry out their threat. I had to say something.

"We weren't—" I began.

But the second foot guard interrupted my protest. "My word," he said, chuckling nastily, "but you two are going to catch it when your parents find out where you've been!"

"Especially as it's the parents that will be held responsible," the first foot guard agreed. "A crime like this could mean the Colonies!" Were they playing with us, or deadly serious? Whatever their game, it was most infuriating, and I wished they would pull all three dogs away.

"You must understand," I blurted out at last. "We need to speak to Lord Chiddingfold."

"Lord who?" The policeman looked completely blank. "I don't think I've ever heard of a Lord *Chiddingfold.*"

"But we need to speak to him urgently on important government business," Beatrice implored.

"Now, look here, missy." The first foot guard leered down at us. "You two are in quite enough trouble as it is. I suggest you come quietly, like you said you would. If you go making up stories, things'll only get worse for the pair of you."

"But we have to speak to Lord Chiddingfold," I insisted, racking my brains for something to say that might make them take us more seriously. "Ask the Prime Minister," I cried hopefully. "He will tell you who we are."

"Oh, so you're friends of the Prime Minister, are you?" the policeman mocked, before snapping, "I think I've had just about enough of this nonsense. You will not be speaking to anyone tonight. You—"

A shout stopped the policeman mid-sentence. A footman was hastening across the lawn towards us, waving an arm above his head. I crossed my fingers and hoped for some miracle that would get us out of this awful mess.

"Now you're in for it!" the first foot guard told us with a sly smile as he patted his agitated hound. "Her Majesty must have seen you. She takes a pretty dim view of intruders, I can tell you." He let out a rasping laugh.

"You never know. She might even chuck you in the Tower!" the police constable added. The three men chortled at the thought, whilst Beatrice and I tried hard to stifle our irritation and anxiety.

As the footman approached, I could see him looking us up and down disapprovingly.

"Her Majesty requests that these children be brought inside," he announced. "She saw them arrive and wishes to question them before you take them away. I am to escort them to the Music Room at once."

The foot guards looked surprised; the policeman even more so. They let us go immediately, their dogs growling with disappointment as we hurried towards the footman. Was this the miracle I had hoped for, I wondered, or we were heading for even deeper water?

We followed the footman across the lawn and in through a small side door next to one of the classical pillars. He ushered us into a darkened room that was lit by two small candles. My eye was drawn to a magnificent unlit chandelier that hung by one thin wire from the middle of a beautiful plaster ceiling rose. Beneath it was a large, shining grand piano. It took me a while to realise that someone was standing beside it. She was small but wore a voluminous black lace-trimmed dress. It was Queen Victoria!

The queen was shorter than I had imagined, and the sour expression on her face filled me with foreboding.

Under normal circumstances I would have been thrilled to meet our great monarch. Now, however, I quite forgot all etiquette. I did not bow but stood dumbstruck in front of the great lady, agonising over what terrible fate might lie ahead of us.

With her eyes still fixed on Beatrice and me, the queen instructed her footman to leave. She waited until the door was firmly closed behind him, then turned towards us and frowned.

"Did you know," she demanded, "that, once upon a time, anyone found entering the palace grounds in the company of a dangerous beast would have been beheaded?"

Beatrice gave a deep curtsey and bowed her head. "We're very sorry, Your Majesty," she said. "We didn't mean any harm."

"You didn't mean any harm, child? Landing a great fire-breathing dragon on the royal lawn? Scaring the royal pets? Had the creature not moved so swiftly, he would even have frightened the life out of my palace guards!"

"It will not happen again, Your Majesty," I promised, remembering my manners at last and bowing as low as I could.

"It had *better* not happen again," the queen retorted, her lips tight with disapproval. Then suddenly her face broke into a kind smile, her eyes twinkled, and she gave a little chuckle. "To be frank," she confided, "we are not accustomed to beheadings these days. They are messy, unpleasant affairs. So it seems that we shall have to pardon you."

I thought I heard Beatrice sigh with relief, and at last my heart slowed to a more regular beat.

"It seems there are only two children in the land who would be so brazen as to land at Buckingham Palace by dragon." She looked at me, then at Beatrice. "I trust I am addressing Daniel and Beatrice Cook, the famous dragonologists?"

We must have stood openmouthed for a whole minute before I finally managed to squeak, "Er, yes, Your Majesty."

"Mr. Gladstone does his best to tell me about the dealings of Lord Chiddingfold, Dr. Drake, and their merry band of dragonologists, but in fact I had never expected to see a dragon with my own eyes, and for that experience, I must thank the two of you."

I was confused. First we were threatened with the Colonies or the Tower, and now the queen was thanking us for breaking into her garden!

"Now, Daniel and Beatrice Cook, I believe that no one else realised there was a dragon with you apart from my royal self, so you are lucky. Which dragon was it, by the way?"

"It was Erasmus, Your Majesty."

"Erasmus—oh, how splendid," cried the queen. "The Guardian's Apprentice! But I do beg your pardon." Her face grew downcast. "You have lost Torcher, your own dragon chick, have you not?"

"How did you know, Your Majesty?" The evening was becoming more peculiar by the moment.

The queen smiled conspiratorially. "Gladstone keeps us informed. The idea that some unknown person has imprisoned a dragon chick is of great concern to the royal household."

"We fear that there is a traitor in the S.A.S.D.," I told her.

"A traitor?" the queen exclaimed. "But who might that be?"

"I'm afraid," Beatrice began carefully, "it's Mr. Tibbs, Your Majesty."

"Mr. Tibbs, Mr. Tibbs, now, let me see. . . ." The queen thought for a moment. "Oh, yes! He is Chiddingfold's private secretary, is he not? A rather sour-faced man? He always looks as though he has just drunk a glass of lime juice and vinegar." She laughed at the thought. "But his credentials are impeccable. You cannot suspect him, surely?"

"I am afraid we have seen proof," I answered gravely. "That is why we need to see Lord Chiddingfold. We need to warn him. It may be Torcher's only hope!"

"His only hope?" the queen repeated. "Then we must call in the constable and have him escort you to Chiddingfold's residence without delay."

The queen stepped over to the fireplace and tugged at an ornately embroidered bellpull. She turned back to speak to us, her face creasing into a kindly smile. "It has been delightful meeting you both. Next time you must stay longer and tell us of your dragon adventures—I gather you have had quite a few of them already. We have heard much of your brave exploits, but I should like to hear more from your own lips. Of that dreadful plague visited upon the naga dragons, how you convinced the hydra to carry you all the way to Jaisalmer, and what the Hong Wei Temple is really like. Oh, there is so much I would love to know!"

"We will gladly return," Beatrice answered, dropping a slight curtsey. "Whenever Your Majesty wishes."

"Then it must be arranged." The queen clapped her hands. "But now I shall wish you good luck. You must go, as they say, with *dragon speed*!"

And with that, the queen called to the footman, who was waiting outside, and instructed him to organise our safe passage to the Chiddingfold residence.

In a matter of moments, we were in a cab being whisked along the Mall with the very same constable who had joked about imprisoning us in the Tower. His attitude was very different now.

"So Her Majesty knows you!" he exclaimed. "And you *are* going to speak to Lord Chiddingfold. What's it all about, then?"

"So now you admit you *have* heard of Lord Chiddingfold?" I asked coldly. I wasn't going to give anything away.

"Of course I have," the constable replied. "It's just that, back in the gardens, I couldn't see what business you two could possibly have with a man of his standing."

A short while later we turned into a square of tall, imposing-looking town houses, and the hansom cab drew to a halt outside a door numbered *22*.

"This is Lord Chiddingfold's residence," said the constable. "Do you need any further assistance?"

Beatrice's eyes narrowed. "Thank you," she answered as we alighted. "But we can manage perfectly well on our own."

The constable ignored her hostility. "Very good, miss, then I'll be on my way." He smiled cheerily and touched his cap. "My name is Gower, by the way. Ask for me next time you find yourselves inconvenienced in the palace gardens. I'll be sure to help."

As the cab clattered away over the cobbles, we climbed the three steps to the large black front door of Lord Chiddingfold's house. I reached for the shiny brass knocker, lifted it, and let it drop. The resounding rap echoed around the square, disturbing the quiet of the night. We waited a few moments, but nobody came.

CHAPTER ELEVEN

THE UNMASKING

Be sure that your armour is well prepared and your
weapons sharp before you head into the lair of the
beast. And remember, fools rush in where brave
knights fear to tread.

—— *Malleus Draconis (The Hammer of the Dragons), Edvardus Rex*

We hammered on Lord Chiddingfold's front door for
a good ten minutes before the rattling and clink-
ing of keys suggested that someone was unlocking it on the
other side. A man in a dressing gown, slippers, and a long
white nightcap opened the door a crack and glared out at us.
I took him to be Lord Chiddingfold's butler.

"Who are you?" he demanded. "Do you realise what
time it is?"

In truth, with everything that had happened, we had
completely lost track of the time. I had not considered for
a moment that the Chiddingfolds might be in bed when we
arrived; my only thought had been to get to the house.

"We are dreadfully sorry," Beatrice answered pleadingly. "We would not disturb you at this late hour were this not a matter of —"

"Life and death!" I interjected.

"We are Beatrice and Daniel Cook," my sister continued, "and we have an urgent message for Lord Chiddingfold."

The butler looked at his pocket watch with obvious irritation. "You will have to come again in the morning after eleven o'clock," he snapped.

"Eleven o'clock?" I wailed. "But that will be too late!"

"Very sorry," the butler said. Then he slammed the door in our faces.

"Blast!" exclaimed Beatrice, turning to me with an exasperated look on her face. "Now what shall we do?"

"Perhaps we should have asked the constable to stay with us after all," I mused.

"But we didn't," snapped Beatrice. "And time's running out. We've got to get to Lord Chiddingfold."

"Billy and Alicia must be inside somewhere," I suggested. "We'll just have to try to make contact with them."

I spotted a few small pebbles by the curbside and bent to pick them up. I clasped one firmly in my right hand and the rest in my left.

"Careful." Beatrice gasped, understanding my intention immediately. "We don't want to get into any more trouble."

"But we can't stand here doing nothing," I retorted.

Leaning back with my right arm behind me, I studied

the windows for clues. The building had four storeys, with some smaller windows high up in the roof.

"Which one do you think I should try first?" I shook the pebble in my right hand in preparation.

"Not the ones at the top," Beatrice said, thinking practically as ever. "Those will be the servants' rooms."

"All right, let's try the third-floor windows. Those are more likely to be family bedrooms."

"I'm not sure I like this idea, Daniel." Beatrice winced slightly. "For goodness' sake, don't damage anything, will you?"

I took aim and flung my arm forward, but the first pebble flew so wide of the mark that it hit a window in the house next door. Next time I concentrated harder, and my aim improved. At last I managed to hit the same third-floor window once, twice, and then a third time.

"Let's just hope it's not the butler's bedroom," Beatrice said.

At last a face appeared at the window. We took a few paces back into the street, but it was difficult to make out the features in the darkness.

"I think it's Billy," cried Beatrice with relief.

I leaned back to throw another stone, but Beatrice caught my arm and held it.

We heard the window creak open and saw someone lean out. "Hey!" came a voice. "You nearly hit me. Who's out there?"

I answered with the S.A.S.D. password. "When a dragon flies . . . ?" I whispered, eager not to disturb the butler again.

"He seeks it with his eyes!" a familiar voice called back. "Daniel, is that you?"

"Yes, Billy, but *shhh,*" I hissed. "We don't want your butler to hear us."

"Sorry," Billy replied in hushed tones. He leaned farther out the window so he could see us properly. "Where on earth have you been?"

"We had to go and see Scramasax," I answered, keeping my voice low. "And now we need to speak to your father urgently."

"But Father is in Wharncliffe," whispered Billy. "He left this morning. He's gone to meet with Brythonnia. He won't be back until tomorrow."

A second head leaned out the window. "There you are!" Alicia cried in a loud whisper. She seemed delighted to see us. "We were all so worried about you. Everyone thought Dragonsbane must have kidnapped you. Mr. Tibbs even came to warn us to stay indoors in case they tried to kidnap us as well."

"Mr. Tibbs?" I exclaimed rather too loudly.

"Shh!" Beatrice put a finger to her lips and gave me a sharp look.

"Yes," Alicia continued. "Father asked him to stay here and keep an eye on us."

"But he mustn't," I cried. "You can't let him. He's a—
a . . . He's a traitor."

"A what?"

Before I could say anything more, a light came on in
the Chiddingfolds' porch, and the front door flew open. A
familiar figure was outlined in the doorway.

"It's Mr. Tibbs!" I called to Beatrice. "Run!" But my own
feet seemed rooted to the spot; Mr. Tibbs rushed towards
me, grabbed me by the collar, and pulled me into the house.
Beatrice backed away, a look of terror on her face.

"Thank goodness you two children are safe!" Mr. Tibbs
exclaimed gruffly.

"Safe?" demanded Beatrice. "What do you mean, 'safe'?"

"From harm, of course," said Mr. Tibbs, perplexed. "Safe
from harm."

Beatrice backed away a little farther.

"Quick!" Mr. Tibbs directed the butler, who was now fully
dressed, with a jerk of his head. "Bring her inside, you fool!
Whatever possessed you to close the door on them earlier?"

The butler ignored Tibbs's question as he advanced
towards Beatrice.

"Run!" I urged.

But the butler was too quick for her. He wrapped a tight
arm around Beatrice's shoulders and steered her inside.
Mr. Tibbs glanced up and down the street with an anxious
expression on his face. He still held me in a viselike grip.

"Are you sure you weren't followed?" he asked with

concern. "You look like you've had the devil's own time." He turned to the butler. "Stay here and make sure that no one enters or leaves the house without my say-so. I need to find out what's been going on."

"Of course, sir," the butler concurred.

"Oh, and hail me a hansom cab," Tibbs ordered.

"Very well, sir." The butler hurried out into the street, whilst Tibbs pushed the door closed and shepherded us into the drawing room.

Beatrice didn't waste any time. "Why did you kidnap Torcher?" she demanded as we turned to face the S.A.S.D. traitor.

"What on earth are you talking about?" Mr. Tibbs looked confused.

"You know very well," snapped Beatrice. "We've found you out. *That's* what I'm talking about."

"I have no idea what you mean," blustered Mr. Tibbs, his concern turning quickly to irritation. A noise in the hallway made him turn just in time to see Billy and Alicia march into the room. By the looks on their faces, they'd understood what I had been trying to tell them about Mr. Tibbs. They eyed him suspiciously, and he seemed to grow more flustered. I was sure he would confess at any moment, but he didn't.

"Why didn't you come straight to me?" he asked, bemused. "I would have helped you."

"Oh really?" I scoffed. "The way you helped us the last time?"

"When you forbade us from visiting the S.A.S.D. head-quarters again?" Beatrice reminded him.

"Ah, yes," he replied. "And I am sorry for it. I truly did not appreciate the gravity of the situation at the time." He sounded genuine, but after we'd been so thoroughly duped by Mr. Anderson, Beatrice and I were having none of it.

"Oh, please stop this deception," said Beatrice. "Just tell us what you are going to do with us."

"*Do* with you?" exclaimed Mr. Tibbs. "I have absolutely no idea what you're talking about. All I know is that I got a message from Lord Chiddingfold saying that you had received a ransom note demanding the Dragon's Claw in return for Torcher. He asked that I keep an eye out for you because Dr. Drake was going to send you back to London after your hurried trip up to Ben Wyvis."

"*You,* keep an eye out for *us?*" Beatrice exploded. "*You?* The very person who kidnapped Torcher and then tried to have us killed! We know the truth. Come on, isn't it time to admit it? *You* are the S.A.S.D. traitor!"

"A traitor?" Tibbs spluttered. "Don't be ridiculous. Why would I want to have you killed? And what possible good would it do me to kidnap Torcher?" His face clouded over. "Has Dr. Drake put you up to this?"

"You had us followed. You wanted to *kill* Scramasax!" I shouted. "You sent that man Anderson with his gun!"

"That's ridiculous!" exclaimed Mr. Tibbs. "You can't kill a dragon with a gun. Even you two should know that."

"Well, Mr. Anderson seemed to think you could," Beatrice said. "And his gun made a big enough hole in the lair. If Daniel hadn't been so brave, neither of us would be here."

"Mr. Anderson had a map of the Dragon Catacombs," I said. "That's how we found you out; we know you gave it to him. And we showed it to Dr. Drake, so he knows the truth now, too, and he's on his way. I shouldn't be surprised if he turns up any minute now, and then you'll be sorry."

"But what do you mean you 'found me out'?" asked Mr. Tibbs, his forehead furrowed in confusion.

"We saw that map on the wall in your office," I cried. "Along with the oath of allegiance to Dragonsbane."

"So that's what you were doing in my office," snapped Mr. Tibbs hotly. "You were spying on me!"

"Yes, and *that's* how we found you out!" Beatrice declared. "We came here to warn Lord Chiddingfold, but we've found you instead." Her tone softened. "So I suppose you have won." She looked dejectedly at the Persian carpet beneath her feet.

"But at least you won't manage to get your hands on the real Dragon's Claw!" I looked him straight in the eye and crossed my arms defiantly.

"Get my hands on the Dragon's Claw?" Mr. Tibbs scratched his head in bewilderment. "This must all be some terrible misunderstanding caused by your impertinent snooping. I admit I should have taken your warning about Torcher more seriously. I may even have begun to change my mind about Dragonsbane. But I don't have the faintest idea who this Mr. Anderson is, and as for his gun, well, that just sounds preposterous."

Beatrice was obviously taken aback by his reaction. "But you did have the map of the Dragon Catacombs, didn't you?"

"Of course I did. I was never sure that Dragonsbane returning was the real reason for the dragon attacks. There is something extremely strange going on, however, and it is clearly connected to their legend. I wanted to find out more about the organisation, and it wasn't difficult to research. It seems that the old Dragon Master Ebenezer Crook was practically obsessed with Dragonsbane. There are whole volumes of his notes on the subject that I found in some old boxes at Wyvern Way—the map was with them."

Beatrice narrowed her eyes, unconvinced. "The copy we saw had been scribbled on in French," said Beatrice. "There were all sorts of instructions. You must have added them for Mr. Anderson."

"In French?" Mr. Tibbs almost laughed at the idea. "I can hardly speak a word!"

Beatrice eyed Mr. Tibbs suspiciously. "Really?" she said.

Alicia cleared her throat softly. "He's telling the truth, Beatrice. We went to Paris a few years ago with Father, and Mr. Tibbs was absolutely hopeless at the language. Worse than Billy, even . . ."

Beatrice hesitated and glanced at me. I was beginning to think that perhaps we'd been too quick to jump to conclusions.

"So the map that you have," I asked, "does it show the entrance to the catacombs?"

"The entrance?" Mr. Tibbs seemed suddenly rather excited. "But that has always been the great mystery about the catacombs. The map doesn't show an entrance at all. Have you found out where it is?"

"We have," I admitted, though I wasn't sure we were ready to give the answer away just yet.

"And this . . . Mr. Anderson . . . had a copy of the map," exclaimed Mr. Tibbs, "but with the entrance marked on it! And he convinced you that he had been sent by me?"

"He had the map," I confirmed. "But he told us Dr. Drake had sent him. He met us on the train just as it was pulling into Edinburgh Station."

"He knew the secret dragonological signs," said Beatrice, "so he must have a connection with someone inside the society! Don't you see? That means there has to be a traitor in the S.A.S.D.!"

"I do," agreed Mr. Tibbs, "but I am most disappointed that you children ever suspected it was me."

It did seem that our suspicions about Mr. Tibbs had been ill founded. "We are sorry," said Beatrice sheepishly. "But you were so angry with us when you banned us from Dr. Drake's Dragonalia, and what with the map and everything we saw the day we visited, it all just seemed to fit together."

"Hmm." I sensed Mr. Tibbs was beginning to understand our point of view.

But if Tibbs wasn't behind all this, who was? My mind was racing now. "So maybe it was Mr. Anderson who left the ransom note," I suggested. "He must have followed us, guessing that we would set off to find the Dragon's Claw straightaway. He was probably on the same train as we were all the way up to Scotland!"

"If he was only after the Dragon's Claw," observed Billy, "then maybe the other attacks have just been diversions."

"I expect Dragonsbane would like to get its hands on all the treasures," said Beatrice. "But it seems there is something especially important about the Dragon's Claw."

Still not completely convinced of Tibbs's innocence, I needed him to answer one more question. "Mr. Tibbs," I said, "when we found you in the room with the copies of the treasures, why were you studying the replica of the Dragon's Claw?"

He showed no hesitation in answering. "Ebenezer Crook's notes describe the Dragon's Claw as a vital key for the Dragonsbane Knights. But he does not say what the key is for."

I was just about to tell Tibbs about the reference to the Claw on Anderson's map when I noticed that Beatrice was becoming agitated. She was looking at an ornate brass clock on the parlour mantelpiece that ticked loudly with each second that passed. "We seem to be forgetting the most important thing in all this," she cried suddenly. "Poor Torcher. We still don't have the Dragon's Claw, and we've only got until ten o'clock this morning to rescue him from his kidnappers, whoever they may be."

"If only Dr. Drake would arrive with the Claw, we could set off and find Torcher now," I said.

"You're right," agreed Mr. Tibbs. Then, sounding a little unsure of himself, he asked, "Do you think you could tell me the whereabouts of the entrance to the catacombs?"

I could no longer see any reason to keep the information to ourselves. "It's at the base of the Lanthorn Tower," I informed him. "You know, at the Tower of London."

"Right," said Tibbs, grabbing his coat and hat. "Let's see if that hansom cab is waiting."

"But we don't have the Dragon's Claw," cried Beatrice. "And we have no idea how long it will take Dr. Drake to bring it to us."

"We do have the replica, however," Mr. Tibbs reminded us. "That will have to do for now. You lot had better wait here, whilst I go to the catacombs to find Torcher. If Dr. Drake arrives, tell him to hurry after me with the real Dragon's Claw!"

"You're going to the Lanthorn Tower alone?" I asked.

"We're coming, too!" exclaimed Beatrice.

Mr. Tibbs's face hardened. "You most certainly are not coming, I cannot expose you to such great danger."

"What about Torcher?" I demanded. "You'll need us to help with him!"

"Have you ever had to look after a dragon chick in London before?" Beatrice continued. "*We* have. It is *not* straightforward! And Torcher trusts us."

"In any case," I added, pulling my hand from my pocket. "I have to give him these." I held up the pieces of flint and iron pyrites that Erasmus had taken from Torcher a few days earlier.

Mr. Tibbs rubbed a hand across his forehead. "Perhaps you are right," he agreed finally. "My studies in dragonology have always been more theoretical than practical. I admit I would not be much use looking after Torcher. I have never really been able to develop a rapport with a real live dragon." He paused to think for a moment. "I would be most grateful for your assistance in caring for Torcher *after* I have saved him. But I shall expect you to follow my every instruction and to stay well back if there is any threat of danger."

"We will," Beatrice and I agreed, relieved to be getting going at last.

"Then we need to make haste."

Tibbs asked Billy and Alicia to wait at the house, ready to inform Lord Chiddingfold and Dr. Drake of our actions. He then rushed out the front door and into the street, where the butler was waiting with the hansom cab. Tibbs beckoned us to follow him.

"Drop us at the entrance to Wyvern Way, please," he told the driver as we all climbed inside. The driver shook the horse's reins and cracked his whip, and before we knew it, we were rattling along Charing Cross Road, then up St. Martin's Lane.

Inside the shop, Mr. Tibbs lit a candle and led us down the stairs into his office in the S.A.S.D. headquarters. By the dim, flickering light of a gas lamp, we sat and waited for him to collect the replica of the Dragon's Claw. His desk was still covered in papers. The map of the Dragon Catacombs was lying on the top of *The Handbook of Hoards*.

Mr. Tibbs pulled out a drawer in his desk and took out an old-fashioned pistol. For an instant, my heart stopped. Was he the traitor after all? But then he saw the expression on my face, smiled, and opened the chamber of the pistol to show me that it was empty.

Tibbs sighed. "I apologise again for not believing you when you first told me about Torcher. But I shall make amends for that mistake, if I can—with this." He held up the gun as he slipped a couple of cartridges into his pocket. "The villains shall not go unpunished!"

"Have you used one of those before?" asked Beatrice anxiously.

"I served my time in the army as a young man," replied Mr. Tibbs as he busied himself about the room, searching for notes and any useful equipment. Finally, he seemed ready. "Time is running out," he told us. "Quickly, check your bags for field supplies and help yourselves to anything you need," Tibbs ordered. "I shall fetch the replica Claw and write a brief note to Dr. Drake. And then we shall head to the Lanthorn Tower."

Chapter Twelve
TRAITORS' GATE

The first place that we must clear of dragons is our capital,
London. For, unknown to the general population, scaled
creatures with the appearance of winged fiends lurk
on the rooftops, defiling our sacred cathedrals and
fouling our lofty palaces.

——*Malleus Draconis (The Hammer of the Dragons), Edvardus Rex*

I t was already early morning as Beatrice and I followed
Mr. Tibbs out of the shop in Wyvern Way. We hurried
after him through the dark streets and down some slippery
steps to the Thames. Ferryboats were already ploughing up
and down the river in the dawn light, and Mr. Tibbs raised
an arm to hail one.

"Where to, guv'nor?" asked the ferryman as we stepped
aboard.

"Traitors' Gate," Mr. Tibbs instructed. "With all the
speed you can muster."

"Traitors' Gate!" The ferryman whistled, then smiled
mischievously as he added, "Is one of these young passengers

having their head chopped off, then? Bit early for that, isn't it?"

"Please just get us there as fast as you can," said Tibbs, impatiently thrusting a coin into the man's hand. "Here is something to lubricate your rowing arms." The ferryman quickly pocketed the half crown and got on with his job quietly.

With each successive bridge we passed, early-morning London seemed more alive. The river was already thick with traffic. Some boats reeked of fish as they sailed towards Billingsgate Market. Then at last we came in sight of the Tower of London. We passed beneath the Tower Wharf and rowed in through the medieval arch known as Traitors' Gate. I shuddered at the thought of the many prisoners who had entered via this gate knowing that they would never be coming out again.

As we moored and climbed the steep steps onto the quay, I looked up at the tower ahead of us. I had not imagined it to be quite so large, or quite so imposing. I stood gazing up for a few moments.

"Over here!" Mr. Tibbs cried, interrupting my thoughts, and I ran to join him and Beatrice. They were heading towards some scaffolding that surrounded what seemed to be a jumbled pile of bricks. The builders had not yet started work that morning, so we were at least free to look around.

"So this is the Lanthorn Tower?" I asked, surprised. It didn't look like much.

"Yes, here it is," said Mr. Tibbs. "It gets its name from the lantern that hung from the top of the tower to guide ships as they came up the river. Originally it was part of the palace of King Henry the Third — Edward Longshanks's father."

So that explained the connection with Dragonsbane.

"I can see no sign of the entrance to the Dragon Catacombs," Mr. Tibbs continued. "It must be well concealed."

"Or hidden by the rubble," I commented. The entrance had remained undiscovered for so long, I wondered what chance we had of finding it.

We searched around the building site, shifting bags of cement and workers' tools, but found nothing. At last, Mr. Tibbs beckoned us to follow him down a short flight of steps. A wooden trapdoor was set into the flagstones at the bottom.

"There," he said with satisfaction. "This must be more or less where the base of the tower once stood. Can you help me lift the door, Daniel?"

I found a crowbar among the tools and used it to lever up the edge of the trapdoor a fraction. Mr. Tibbs slid a hand underneath to pry it up. It was heavy, but once he had his weight behind it, he managed to fling it open with ease. Tibbs eagerly looked inside, then sighed with disappointment. "It doesn't seem to be anything more than an empty store chamber." He gazed around. It was difficult to see much in the underground darkness. "Wait — maybe there's a way out that I can't see from here."

He climbed down the ladder that led into the chamber.

Beatrice and I followed him. We could just make out dim outlines in the basement gloom.

"You see?" said Mr. Tibbs. "There's nothing here."

"Then what is that stack of torches doing there?" I asked.

"That's strange, too," said Beatrice, pointing towards a huge carving on one of the walls. It was in the shape of a shield and decorated with three lions.

"What's so strange about it? It's medieval, and we're in a medieval building," I said.

"Yes, but this is just an underground storeroom. Why would they bother to decorate it with a fancy carving like this?" She put her hand flat on her head and measured herself against the shield. Look — it's much bigger than I am."

"You're right: this *is* an odd place for such an impressive carving," agreed Mr. Tibbs, hurrying across to examine the shield. As he ran his finger over the lions, a sudden thought sprang into my mind.

"The map!" I cried. "Mr. Anderson's map. It had a note attached to it — don't you remember? It said something about lions and eyes and tongues, didn't it?"

"Yes," said Beatrice. "Of course it did." She thought for a moment, then said, " 'Press the eyes and pull the tongue.' Wasn't that it?" I nodded eagerly as she joined Mr. Tibbs in front of the carving. "Let's see if it works on these lions."

The lions on the shield had ugly, bulging eyes, but none of them seemed to have a tongue. Beatrice's hand hovered in front of the topmost lion; she tried jabbing two fingers into its eye sockets. For a moment nothing happened, then there was a sudden click, and a tongue shot out from the mouth of the middle lion. We all nearly jumped out of our skins! Beatrice gave a little cry and just stood there, not knowing what to do next.

"Now you'll have to pull it," I urged. Why was she being so slow?

"What do you think will happen?" she asked fearfully.

"We won't know until we try it, will we?" I answered. At last Beatrice gave the protruding tongue a sharp tug and pulled it right out of the lion's mouth, to discover that it was attached to the shield by a long chain. Beatrice let go of the stone tongue again, and with another click, the shield swung silently inwards, like a stone door, revealing a dark passage-way beyond. Straightaway I moved to step inside.

"Wait!" cried Mr. Tibbs. He hurriedly picked up one of the torches and fumbled to light it. "Let me go first. We don't know what's on the other side."

With the benefit of the torchlight, I peered into the passageway once more—and gasped. In the flickering light, I could now see that the tunnel was stacked high with bones—thousands upon thousands of them.

"It's full of bones!" I exclaimed, shuddering at the sight of the huge white skulls that jutted menacingly into the passageway.

Beatrice tutted and gave me a look. "Of course it is! That's what catacombs are, silly. This particular catacomb

must be an underground cemetery for dead dragons." She peered inside. "And it gives me the jitters," she added.

I knew what Beatrice meant. I felt a shiver run right through me as I surveyed the bones. "So this is the work of Dragonsbane?"

"I'm afraid so," Mr. Tibbs answered. "This is where the Dragonsbane Knights piled up the bones of the dragons they slaughtered. Down here in these cool, damp conditions, the bones could last for thousands of years."

"The lost dragons of Britain," I marveled.

Beatrice hugged her arms about herself. "Who could have imagined there were so many!"

"Indeed, there were many thousands of them before the last great dragon slaying," Mr. Tibbs confirmed sombrely.

I swallowed. "And now Dragonsbane has returned to finish the job," I said.

"Well, someone is trying to finish the job," Mr. Tibbs answered. He seemed to still not be convinced by the Dragonsbane theory. He handed the torch to Beatrice, illuminating some carved lettering above the entrance to the catacombs as he did so. We paused to examine it.

"*'Bienvenue au Royaume des Dragons Morts,'*" Mr. Tibbs read.

"It's in French again." Beatrice translated the words in a whisper: "'Welcome to the Kingdom of Dead Dragons'!" The words chilled us each to the core, but now was not the time to contemplate the horror of the place: we had a living dragon to rescue.

Mr. Tibbs handed the torch to Beatrice and spread out the map on the floor of the chamber. We knelt down to take a closer look.

"If this is accurate, it will lead us through the Dragon Catacombs." Mr. Tibbs smoothed out the creases with his hand and pointed to some writing in the middle. "To the central chamber: the Grand Lodge of Dragonsbane."

Beatrice leaned forward to study the map. "I expect there will be more puzzles to solve, like the one that opened the shield."

"In truth, we must be extremely careful," warned Mr. Tibbs, "for those will not be marked on the map. The Dragonsbane Knights clearly went to some lengths to keep their headquarters both secret and safe. We have no idea how many traps they may have positioned about the place, or indeed whether any of them are still working. You two must walk directly behind me. Try to tread in my footsteps if you can."

Beatrice handed back the torch, and we set off into the labyrinth, one in front of the other. My sister and I took bold strides to match our step with that of Mr. Tibbs. It felt eerie to be walking between the dry bones of so many dead dragons. Worse still, all the tunnels looked the same; before long, I had lost any sense of direction. Beatrice was obviously in the same boat. "We had better keep tight hold of the map," she said. "If we were to lose it, I imagine we'd be stuck in here forever." We surveyed the tunnels and the bones that flanked them.

"Perhaps we should have brought a big ball of string to roll out behind us, like Theseus in the labyrinth of the Minotaur," I joked.

"It would have to be a very long ball of string," Mr. Tibbs commented. "We must have travelled a quarter of a mile already."

Beatrice joined in our banter. "If only we had brought some bread, we could have dropped crumbs behind us like Hansel and Gretel." At least it kept our minds from the horrors that might lie ahead of us.

"I suspect any crumbs would be eaten by the rats," Mr. Tibbs said with a grimace.

"Rats!" exclaimed Beatrice with a shiver. "I do wish you hadn't said that." Gingerly, she pulled a bone from the top of one of the stacks. "We could use some of these ribs to mark the tunnels that we pass. Then at least we'd know which ones we took and which we didn't."

"It seems somehow disrespectful," I answered.

"Do you really think the dead dragons will mind?" Beatrice retorted, laying a large tibia bone along the entrance of the next tunnel we passed. "We are facing the same enemy, remember. And we can always put the bones back on the way out."

After another hundred yards or so, the tunnel became wider. Mr. Tibbs held the torch aloft, and we gazed up at the ceiling. It was covered in coloured dots that looked strangely beautiful, sparkling in the torchlight—until we realised what they were.

"They're jewels," cried Beatrice. "But they look like eyes!"

Mr. Tibbs nodded and spoke uneasily, "The eyes of the dead. Two for each dragon slain. That must mean we are nearing the central chamber. We should take great care from here onwards." He lowered his torch and then suddenly stopped dead with an angry cry.

I rushed forwards to see what was wrong.

"No, don't move, either of you," he ordered. "I think I just caught something with my foot. Oh, goodness." He paused.

"What is it?" asked Beatrice nervously.

"I don't know for certain," Mr. Tibbs answered. "But it could have been a tripwire."

"You mean we've walked into a trap?" I cried, my heart thumping.

Mr. Tibbs nodded slowly. "I fear that is exactly what it is. Look behind you," he said through gritted teeth.

We turned to look back along the tunnel. At the point where it started to widen, a clear liquid was slowly trickling from the ceiling. The liquid hissed as it dribbled over the stacked-up bones of the dragons. An acrid smoke rose up and was drifting towards us.

"Ugh! It's coming from the eyes!" wailed Beatrice. "It's dissolving the bones as it touches them."

"The tears of acid!" I cried. "Beatrice, they were mentioned on Anderson's map. Do you remember the instruction?" But gradually, as the smoke began to fill our nostrils, it became harder to breathe, let alone speak. Beatrice started to cough.

"Try to cover your mouth and nose," Mr. Tibbs shouted as he struggled not to cough.

Now the acid had turned from a few trickles on the walls to a thick spray that moved towards us like a cloud along the ceiling.

"Quickly!" said Mr. Tibbs. "We must keep going."

We turned the next corner, only to be confronted with another acid cloud approaching from the opposite end of the tunnel. We lowered ourselves to the floor, as the air was clearer there. Our throats and eyes continued to sting, however. It was hardly possible to breathe, let alone think of a way out of this dreadful trap. My mind continued whirring nevertheless.

"Look . . . for some . . . dragons' . . . heads," I coughed.

"What?" answered Mr. Tibbs, spluttering as he spoke.

"We have to . . . shut one of the eyes, or something. . . ." I gasped, but the acid burned all the more. "It . . . said so on . . . the map."

"'*Fermez l'oeil rouge*' . . ." croaked Beatrice, trying to remember the words she had translated the previous day.

Mr. Tibbs looked around wildly for some dragons' heads. "There . . . are none," he tried to shout. By now the acid clouds that approached us from either end of the tunnel had reached halfway. The smoke grew thicker by the moment.

"Look—look behind—the stacks—of bones," cried Beatrice between coughs.

Mr. Tibbs gave the torch to Beatrice and scrambled up frantically onto one of the stacks. The acid cloud was thicker there, and he coughed uncontrollably for a few moments before gaining his composure and pulling his jacket over his mouth for protection. He began scooping knucklebones from the top of the pile. "This will take too long," he cried.

Beatrice took out a handkerchief to cover her mouth; she pulled mine from my pocket and handed it to me. But she wobbled as she did so, and the torch swung away from her momentarily, illuminating another pile of bones. Something caught my eye.

I gestured to Beatrice to swing the torch back towards the other pile. Three dragon skulls had been fixed to the front of the huge stack of bones. I had noticed something green glinting out of one of the eye sockets.

"The eyes!" I struggled to speak. "What . . . was it about them?"

"I . . . think we have to . . . close them." Beatrice coughed. By now the acid cloud had nearly reached us. The hissing of dissolving bones had turned into a deafening roar, and I could barely see through the tears that streamed from my stinging eyes.

I covered the green gem with my hand. Nothing happened. If anything, the acid seemed to advance more quickly.

From the corner of my eye, I could see Beatrice waving her arms, the torchlight swinging eerily about the tunnel. What was she trying to say? I could barely hear her. I tried to ignore the roar of the acid. Through the smoke I could just see her lips moving.

"*'Fermez l'oeil rouge,'*" she was saying. "Red . . . not green!"

"Of course!" I could have kicked myself. I hurried to the next head. There was another green gem. On to the next. A red gem! I slapped my hand over it angrily. The acid shower stopped in an instant. I took my hand away. It started again.

"What are you doing?" Beatrice tried to shout, but her voice came out as a hoarse whisper. "Cover it up!"

There had to be some sort of light beam that connected to the gem and activated the acid supply. When I stopped the acid, I could think and breathe more clearly. I needed to keep the gem covered. With my hand still in position, I took the handkerchief from my mouth to breathe in the clearing air. Of course! I screwed it up and stuffed it into the eye socket of the dragon skull.

"It's working," I cried. "Let's get out of here quickly!" I swung my foot forwards, but a hand grabbed my shoulder.

"Wait!" Mr. Tibbs warned. Looking down, I could see the liquid acid swirling on the ground. The cloud had dispersed, but the acid continued dribbling to the floor. We waited a few moments, and it gradually seeped away, leaving nothing but the gently steaming remains of the bones that once lined the booby-trapped corridor.

Mr. Tibbs took back the torch and we continued on, stepping carefully, one behind the other, to avoid any remaining pools of acid. The tunnel turned a corner, and I leaned over to see beyond Mr. Tibbs. I wondered what lay ahead of us now.

"There are a couple of things in front of the doors up ahead." I pointed. "Can you see what they are?"

Beatrice craned her neck to see better. "Statues, I think." She screwed up her eyes to focus on them. Mr. Tibbs lowered the torch to improve our light. "They look like medieval knights."

"It could be another trap," I suggested.

"I do hope not," Beatrice said. "We have no more clues to tell us how to get past them."

A short while later, we were standing in front of the two imposing statues. The stone knights were portrayed in full armour with real swords raised—one on either side of the tunnel—as if they might strike anyone who passed between them. Each had a banner above his head, one bearing the name "Norfolk," the other "Northumberland." I strode forwards to examine them.

"Daniel, stop!" Mr. Tibbs shouted. "This might be a trap, remember. We must tread carefully and try to find a trip-switch."

"A what?" I asked, perplexed.

"A trip-switch. It's something that you might step on without realising that could activate those statues. See how sharp the swords are? If one swung down upon us, I dread to think what the consequence would be."

We searched carefully but found nothing.

"You two wait here," Mr. Tibbs instructed. "Let me see if I can get past."

"Oh, do be careful, Mr. Tibbs," Beatrice urged.

With the torch held out in front of him, he flattened himself against the statue to ensure that a descending sword would not strike him. Looking up and down the statue all the while, he began inching past it. Nothing happened. Using his left foot, he felt for any tripwires or switches as he worked his way across to the other side. He moved slowly, checking methodically for unseen devices, until finally he had passed right across the statue.

"Well done!" cried Beatrice

Mr. Tibbs wiped his brow with relief. "Now you two try!" he instructed. "But be careful. Move as gently as you possibly can, feeling ahead of you all the time. The switch may just be stuck."

I held my breath as Beatrice made her way very gradually past the two statues. She reached the other side safely, and I followed her, my heart hammering in my chest as I pushed my way slowly across.

"We've done it!" I cried once I had joined the others on the far side of the statues.

But the challenge was not over yet. We now stood in front of four doors. In the centre of each was a thin slot about five inches wide. Two of the doors were decorated with images of knights dressed in medieval armour—one red and one green; the other two with images of dragons—one red and one green. A message, painted in red above all four doors, read, *"Choisissez avec soin."*

"'Choose with care,'" Beatrice translated. "But *how* do we choose?"

"I don't know," I answered, thinking hard. "If only we'd kept the other map. We should never have let Dr. Drake take it!"

"But we had no idea we were coming to the catacombs," Beatrice replied. "And in any case, Dr. Drake should have been here by now."

Mr. Tibbs had been silent for a while. He was marching slowly to and fro in front of the doors, then looking back at the statues. He stroked his chin with one hand and held the torch in the other. Suddenly, he slotted the torch into a bracket on the wall and strode towards one of the statues.

"I'm sure the slots give us some sort of clue," he said. "They seem just deep enough to fit a sword blade."

"Good thinking, Mr. Tibbs!" cried Beatrice, following him back to the statue.

He tugged at a sword one of the statues held, and it slipped gently out of the knight's hand. He fetched the other just as easily.

"Now all we have to do is figure out which sword goes in which slot," Beatrice declared.

"Hmm." Mr. Tibbs gave a wistful smile. "You make it sound such a simple task."

"Well, I'm sure there is a simple solution," Beatrice insisted.

"Perhaps they are coded," I suggested. "The colours green and red might mean something."

"How about green for go and red for danger?" Beatrice proposed.

"Or red could be the colour of Saint George, the patron of the Dragonsbane Knights," I argued.

"What about the lettering above the door?" said Beatrice. " *'Choisissez avec soin.'* The letters are in red. Perhaps that is the clue we are looking for."

"But what if we get it wrong?" I said.

I could see Tibbs was getting impatient. "Then we shall have to face the consequences," he snapped. "We don't have much time left to save Torcher." His words made perfect sense.

"All right," I agreed. "Let's try it."

"Stand back," Mr. Tibbs ordered. He pushed one of the swords into the slot in the red knight's door, and it slid home with a click. He did the same with the red dragon's door. There was another click, and then both doors swung open, revealing a further length of tunnel, with dragon's-head statues flanking its walls.

"Oh, well done!" Beatrice cried, clapping her hands and jumping up and down.

"There," Mr. Tibbs said. "That wasn't so difficult, now, was it?"

He stooped to collect the torch, and we set off purposefully along the new tunnel.

"What's that on the floor?" I asked. It seemed blanketed in a pitch-black powder.

"It looks like soot," Beatrice observed as Mr. Tibbs lowered the torch for us to see better.

We heard a dull thud and turned just in time for the doors to swing shut behind us. Beatrice ran back and pushed hard against them. "They won't budge," she cried in panic.

Suddenly there came a distant rustling, crackling sound. The mouths of the dragon's-head statues glowed red and orange, then spat out tongues of flame, which illuminated the gloomy tunnel with a startling light. The noise grew deafening.

"Oh, no!" I exclaimed. "We must have chosen the wrong doors after all!"

"And we don't even have water to put out the fire!" Mr. Tibbs shouted above the din.

Beatrice was fumbling in her backpack. "We've no time to mess about now," I told her. "Think of something we can do!"

"But I have thought of something," she retorted, holding a crumpled heap of dragon skin in her hand.

"Of course!" I exclaimed. "The flameproof cloaks! Bea, you are a genius."

"Quick," Beatrice yelled, pulling her cloak over her head. "Both of you — get under here!" I paused, thinking of getting my own cloak from my pack, but there was no time.

We threw ourselves beneath the cloak and huddled together with our backs to the wall as the flames belching from the dragon statues intensified. The heat in the tunnel soon became unbearable, and we gasped for water. The cloak, however, did not even begin to char.

Then, all at once, the crackling noise stopped, the flames receded as quickly as they had begun, and the doors at the far end of the tunnel creaked open. The three of us were left dry-mouthed and panting for breath, but our relief was enormous.

"Thank goodness we packed the cloak!" Beatrice exclaimed. "Or we would surely have been incinerated!"

"We'd have been reduced to soot," I agreed.

"What a dreadful thought," Mr. Tibbs interjected. "We have answered one question, though."

"Oh?" I couldn't think what he was referring to.

"Now we know where the soot came from!"

We rushed through the open doors, and they closed swiftly behind us.

"I wonder which of the four doors would have gotten us through safely." Beatrice was thinking aloud, but all at once everything seemed to click into place in my mind, and I was sure I knew the answer.

"Imagine you were a Dragonsbane Knight," I told her

eagerly. "You would know what to do without having to think for a moment."

"Really?" Beatrice looked puzzled. "What would that be?"

"Well, colour has nothing to do with it," I explained. "We were trying too hard. A Dragonsbane Knight would have stabbed the swords straight into the two dragons instantly."

I waited for Beatrice to congratulate me on my brilliance, but she just sighed and muttered, "If only you'd thought of that sooner."

We continued along the tunnel, placing crossed ribs wherever we found a junction and keeping a close eye on the map. Gradually, the tunnel widened until we seemed almost to be *inside* the body of an enormous dragon. The ceiling was covered in large scales, like those one might find on a dragon's back, whilst the floor was made up of hundreds of coloured tiles shaped like the scales on its belly.

Mr. Tibbs came to a sudden halt in front of us, stretching his arms wide so we could not surge past him. "Let us not be hasty," he said as his eyes darted around the room, taking in every detail.

"Do you think this is another puzzle?" asked Beatrice. "The scales all seem to have runes on them."

"Perhaps we should just run across them quickly," I suggested.

Mr. Tibbs gasped in horror. "No, no, no!" he cried. "If you tread on the wrong scales, they will almost certainly activate another trap."

We all stood still as statues and looked about the chamber for any possible clues. Gazing upwards, I pointed out a sign on the ceiling painted in red runes. It read, *"Mort aux dragons!"*

Our hearts sank. "I think that means it *is* another puzzle." Beatrice sighed.

There was something underneath the sign that seemed to have faded with age. We looked more closely until we could just make out a picture of a red dragon holding a carved scroll in its mouth. Mr. Tibbs took a tentative step towards it and held up the torch. There was writing underneath. He read aloud: " 'Just but valiant knight, walk with care on that which is missing from this quizzically exquisite puzzle.' "

"At least it's in English this time," I said. "But it doesn't make any sense."

"What on earth does it mean by 'that which is missing'?" Beatrice queried.

"How can you walk on something that isn't there?" I wondered aloud.

"Maybe it has something to do with the letters in the instruction," Beatrice answered. "But the sentence seems to contain all the letters of the alphabet. I can see *x, y,* and *z* as well as *q* and *u.* They're normally the less common letters."

"Or perhaps the item is missing from the floor," ventured Mr. Tibbs, holding the torch out in front of him to study the pattern of scales. We followed his gaze.

"There's an *A*-rune, a *B*-rune, a *C*-rune," I noticed. "And I can see an awful lot of *D*-runes."

"*D* for *Dragonsbane,*" commented Beatrice. I looked back to the sign on the wall.

"That's it!" I cried. "The clue is in the sentence after all. It doesn't contain the letter *D*. That's what's missing!"

"My goodness, you're right!" Mr. Tibbs laughed, visibly impressed by my powers of deduction. "There is even a pattern of *D*-runes, if you look carefully, that stretches all the way from here to the other side!"

"It must be a path!" Beatrice exclaimed. "Shall we try it?"

Mr. Tibbs nodded thoughtfully. "Yes, but we must be very careful," he warned. "Let's move one step at a time. And get ready to jump back quickly if anything happens."

We studied the *D*-rune path carefully and readied ourselves for the trial. Mr. Tibbs gripped the torch firmly. "I shall go first again," he told us. "If nothing happens to me, then you two should follow my steps exactly."

There was a gap before the first scale, and Mr. Tibbs had to stride across to it. I held my breath, but he reached it with no trouble — no jets of acid or flaming dragons' tongues this time! As he held up the torch, the path before us became clearer — and it seemed to offer no further challenges.

He stepped back a few paces to the edge of the first scale and held out an arm. "*D*-runes it is, then." He sighed with relief. "Now, Beatrice, grab my arm and jump across."

She took a deep breath and reached Mr. Tibbs easily. I followed. The scales were large, but with all three of us standing on just one of them, we were rather squashed.

"Good." Mr. Tibbs sounded a little more relaxed now. "You two hold on to each other, whilst I step on a few paces, then I'll wait for you to join me."

He moved forwards slowly at first but built up speed as he grew more confident of the path. At last he turned and called back, "It's working! Follow my route exactly!"

Before too long, we had walked nearly the length of the chamber and crossed to the other side of the scales. We moved timidly, however, afraid that stepping on one wrong scale could unleash unimaginable horrors. It was damp and cold in the tunnel, but I felt warm as toast from concentrating so hard.

"Phew," said Beatrice, mopping her face with her hand-kerchief. "We've made it."

I looked back across the winding path we had just followed. It was a relief to be on the other side, but I couldn't help wondering what would have happened had we chosen differently. Before I could stop myself, I tapped one of the C-rune scales with my toe.

"Daniel, what are you doing?" cried Beatrice. But it was too late. With a sudden *whoosh,* a section of tiles dropped away, leaving a yawning hole in the middle of the floor. I jumped away in shock, but then couldn't help leaning over to look inside the hole. Far below was a deep, water-filled pit. The jagged tips of deadly spears and lances protruded from its surface.

"You foolish boy!" Mr. Tibbs snapped, turning puce with rage. "I knew I should never have brought you children with me."

"You might not have found the route across the scales if it wasn't for me," I retorted. But I knew he was right. I had behaved stupidly.

"Well, there's no way we can go back along that path now," Mr. Tibbs snarled. "We shall have to find an alternate exit." But curiosity got the better of him, and for a moment he too leaned over the pit to take a look inside.

"I don't know what came over me," I said.

"Well, let us at least hope you have learned a lesson from this," Mr. Tibbs said with a sigh. "And make sure it does not happen again."

As we continued silently along the maze of tunnels, Mr. Tibbs marched angrily ahead of us. I could tell Beatrice was also cross with me, and I wallowed in self-pity. I hated that anyone should think I was a fool.

Since we could no longer return the way we had come, there seemed little point in placing bones at the tunnel junctions. Thankfully, we encountered no further traps, however, and at last the tunnel opened into a lofty chamber, hung with flaming torches that blinded our eyes with their sudden, startling light. They also made my heart thump. Who was here? I wondered. Who had lit them?

Mr. Tibbs stopped to study the map. "We have arrived," he said at last, "in the antechamber of the Grand Lodge of Dragonsbane: the robing room!"

Beatrice sniffed the air. "It smells of dragon!" she cried

eagerly. I could pick up the familiar sulphurous odour, too. It wasn't exactly pleasant, but my mood lifted immediately.

"Perhaps Torcher is nearby," I said. I felt excited and hopeful at last.

"What do we do now?" asked Beatrice.

Mr. Tibbs advanced towards a gigantic pair of doors at the opposite end of the chamber. "Stay behind me," he instructed firmly. "And keep quiet. I am going to open one door a fraction to see what is on the other side. If anyone is there, then at least I have my pistol." He patted his pocket. "I think we can leave the torch here now. And you two should take the map. If anything happens to me, then you must do your best to escape and raise the alarm."

"What if there's no one there?" I asked.

"Then, with luck, that means the coast is clear, and we can try to find Torcher without being discovered."

Beatrice and I watched anxiously as Mr. Tibbs made his way over to the doors. On his approach, they swished open. He stiffened a little, and I saw him feel for the pistol in his jacket, but he kept walking, turning back cautiously to look in our direction. "I can't see anyone inside," he hissed.

"Then who opened the doors?" asked Beatrice under her breath.

Mr. Tibbs shrugged and made to continue, but then we heard a sharp cry, followed by a low, rumbling whine: the distinct sound of a dragon in pain. Mr. Tibbs hurried on through the doors.

Beatrice gasped. "It's Torcher. I'm sure of it!"

All at once we ran, unthinking, through the doors and entered a magnificent circular hall. Its domed ceiling was intricately decorated, and its walls were adorned with ornate carvings and paintings of dragons. An array of thronelike seats faced inwards in a broad circle. At the far end, rearing up on its hind legs as if about to attack, was a magnificent statue of a European dragon, resplendent with golden scales. Rubies sparkled from its eye sockets, and its outspread wings all but touched the ceiling.

"Look," I said, pointing at the gigantic statue. "One of its foreclaws is missing. It looks as though the Dragon's Claw would fit in that socket perfectly."

"I don't think so," Beatrice scoffed. "The Dragon's Claw is from a Chinese *lung* dragon, not a European dragon."

"I am sure Dragonsbane would not have worried about such details." Mr. Tibbs gave an ironic laugh. "To them, a dragon was just a dragon. It was their enemy and deserved to die."

The dragon cries seemed to have stopped, and the hall fell eerily quiet—but not for long. All at once a disembodied voice addressed us. It echoed around the hall, seeming almost to come from the mouth of the great dragon statue.

"Greetings, strangers!" the voice boomed. "Or perhaps we are not such strangers after all. I had not thought to see

you here." It paused dramatically. "We had an appointment at the Eleanor Cross, did we not? And, Daniel and Beatrice, I see that you have disobeyed my orders to tell no one of your mission." As it grew angry, the voice crescendoed. Then it dropped back and gave a bitter laugh. "With only Mr. Tibbs to escort you, I am surprised you have survived the dangers of the labyrinth. But now that you are here, I do so hope that you have brought me the Dragon's Claw. I can hardly bear to think what I shall have to do to you should you not have it with you."

"Who are you?" cried Beatrice boldly. "Show yourself!"

"I am the Master of the Secret Order of Dragonsbane Knights," the voice announced. "Now, show me the Claw!"

"Not until we see who you are!" retorted Beatrice.

"You are in no position to bargain with me." He seemed surprised, almost amused.

Mr. Tibbs took the replica Dragon's Claw from his pack and held it up. I could see he was getting into one of his tempers, his face reddening and the veins on his temples throbbing. "Where is Torcher?" he demanded, the level of his voice reaching a pitch that rivalled the fury of the disembodied voice.

"Oh, he's over there." The voice was calm, dismissive, and uncaring now. "Look to the portcullis beneath the portrait of Saint George," it said. "That is where you will find him."

We saw the painting immediately and rushed to grasp the bars of the great portcullis. Tibbs banged on them in frustration so that they rattled and creaked, but the sound did not disturb the little dragon that lay behind them. Tears blurred my vision when I saw Torcher. Our happy, playful dragon chick was lying on his side, hardly moving at all. His eyes were closed, his scaly neck bound with a thick iron chain that was fixed to the wall behind him.

"You beast!" Beatrice cried. "What have you done to him?"

"Oh, he has merely been pacified," said the voice. "But the question is not what I *have done* to him so much as what I am *going* to do to him. And that all depends on you."

With each syllable it uttered, the voice seemed to grow more familiar. I was sure I had heard it before, but for the life of me, I could not think where. The man behind it certainly knew the three of us. Was this the S.A.S.D. traitor?

"Hold out the Claw, Tibbs," the voice commanded.

Mr. Tibbs did as he was ordered. Somewhere in the distance, we heard a rumble of ancient machinery. Slowly, squeaking and grinding as it moved, the portcullis rose a couple of feet from the ground.

Beatrice and I rushed forwards.

"Don't go in there!" warned Mr. Tibbs. "It could be a trap!"

But it was too late. Beatrice and I had slipped under the grille and were at Torcher's side in a moment. The poor little chick was barely breathing. We petted and stroked him, but he hardly responded at all.

"Look at him!" Beatrice said, tears on her face. "He's only barely alive!"

Meanwhile, the voice continued to boom around the hall. "Tibbs," it commanded, "place the Dragon's Claw in the socket of the statue."

Mr. Tibbs shook the Claw in his hand. I knew he was trying to think of a way out of the situation, but as far as I could see, there was none. After our ordeals in the tunnels, we were all well aware of what "the voice" was capable of doing. Tibbs stamped across to the dragon statue and forced the replica Claw into the socket.

"Now pull the Dragon's Claw towards you."

Mr. Tibbs tried to pull the Claw forward, but nothing happened: the rest of the arm did not even move.

"Try again, Tibbs," the voice commanded impatiently.

"I cannot," said Mr. Tibbs.

"What do you mean 'cannot'?" It seemed the voice was reaching the limits of its patience. "Don't you mean *will* not?"

There was something more familiar about the menacing anger of its tone. I screwed up my eyes and concentrated hard. And suddenly I realised who the voice belonged to. It was a man whom we had all believed dead.

"That's not the Master of Dragonsbane," I cried. "It's Ignatius Crook!"

The voice did not respond, but the portcullis creaked and groaned and slammed to the ground before I could move a muscle. Beatrice and I were trapped.

CHAPTER THIRTEEN
THE GOLDEN HOARD

*Failure to slay dragons will be regarded as treachery
by the king. Those knights who do not succeed in
their quest must face the consequences. They will be
given a stark choice: exile or death.*

—— *Malleus Draconis (The Hammer of the Dragons), Edvardus Rex*

Ignatius Crook stepped from behind the statue of the
dragon, yet I could still recognise him only by his voice.
He was swathed in a long, black cloak with a deep hood that
covered much of his face.

In fury, Mr. Tibbs drew his pistol and pointed it in
Crook's direction. His hand was shaking, either from fear or
rage; I could not tell which.

"Put down that gun, Tibbs," said Ignatius wearily. "You
know you are not man enough to use it, even to save these
irritating children whom I thought you despised."

Tibbs steadied his hand and kept the pistol aimed firmly
at Crook. "We will see about that," Mr. Tibbs snarled.

"We thought you were dead, Ignatius," I shouted through the portcullis bars, and in truth, at that moment I wished he was.

"Dead?" Ignatius laughed. "Ha! So Captain Hezekiah's tale has spread, has it? After he abandoned me on the Island of Dragons. Abandoned me . . . to *this*!"

Ignatius threw back his hood. His face and hands were covered with ugly skin blisters, and in parts his flesh seemed almost to have melted to his bones. I would hardly have recognised him now, even without the hood of his cloak — were it not for the voice.

Ignatius told us his story, as though he somehow imagined us a sympathetic audience.

"Hezekiah was right about the island's evil amphithere," he said. "It attacked me and left me for dead. Indeed, I would have died had I not had the presence of mind to fashion myself a raft, on which I made my escape. Six days and nights I floated upon that pile of rotten tree branches, until a Spanish ship picked me up and brought me back to Europe."

According to Ignatius, his father had spent the best part of his life, not to mention the entire family fortune, in pursuit of the secrets of Dragonsbane and in a desperate search for the Lost Island of Dragons. He was convinced that, one day, the greatest-ever threat to dragons would come from there.

Ebenezer Crook was never able to pay a visit himself, but an old cartographer's globe that showed the precise location of the island had encouraged Ignatius on his mission.

The family home had burned down just over one year earlier. Ignatius was still smarting from his father's refusal to pass on the title of Dragon Master to him after his death, and now, because of the fire, Ignatius had lost any further inheritance he might have claimed.

"And so you travelled to the island to search for gold to make up for your family's lost fortune?" I remarked. It was typical of Ignatius to seek compensation for his loss from a source over which he had no claim. I was appalled, but I was also playing for time. I hoped that if I kept Ignatius talking, then either Dr. Drake would find us or one of us would come up with an escape plan.

"I am sure there is gold aplenty on the island, but I did not find a single sovereign," Ignatius continued, his tone bitter and resentful. "The guardian amphithere saw to that."

But Ignatius had found one thing on the island that he could use to his advantage: a wand charged with some special sort of dragon dust that gave power over basilisks. On his return, he had hit upon a plan.

"It was when I read about the rebuilding of the Lanthorn Tower," he explained. "I knew that I would finally be able to get into the catacombs, with the help of one useful thing my father had left behind for me—a map." It seemed that, shortly before his death, Ebenezer Crook had found a description of the catacomb traps concealed among some old papers that were reputed to have belonged to the Earl of Northumberland. He had even unravelled a puzzle that told him where the entrance lay. He had died a few months later, before having a chance to pass his knowledge on to the S.A.S.D., though a folded copy of the map of the catacombs lay at his bedside when he died. He had added notes to it that explained how to gain safe entry and overcome the booby traps.

"Dragonologists are such fools," Ignatius scoffed. "I realised that with a few well-timed attacks and some silly rings I had made, it would be easy to convince them that the deadly Dragonsbane Knights had returned to wreak vengeance on dragonkind! In fact, my intention was merely to get the likes of Dr. Drake and your meddling parents out of the way. I knew that my easiest route to the Dragon's Claw was through you two children and your soppy attitude to that dragon chick."

Ignatius had found recruits for the new Order of Dragonsbane Knights easily, by promising gold and offering a unique experience: the chance to hunt a real live dragon.

"So that's how Anderson got involved!" I exclaimed.

"Anderson?" Ignatius chuckled. "Oh, you mean Major Wilson, the famous big-game hunter. He's a mercenary fellow, isn't he?" Apparently, Ignatius had invited the major to visit him in the catacombs. He had sent Ebenezer's map and instructed the major to bring his gun. Having proved to Ignatius that it was indeed powerful enough to kill a dragon, the major had learned a few secret signs and a password or two.

Then Ignatius had given him his instructions and sent him off to follow us.

"But why do you want the Dragon's Claw?" asked Beatrice, her hand still gently stroking Torcher's brow.

Ignatius's disfigured face cracked into a warped smile. "The Dragonsbane Knights were careful men. They hid their many, many riches well."

"So, the Claw is the key to releasing the gold!" I realised.

"And that is all this whole thing has been about?" Beatrice was disgusted.

"Do you realise, foolish child, exactly how much gold is hidden behind these walls? The Dragonsbane Knights were rich even beyond *my* wildest dreams!"

"You're welcome to their treasure," snapped Beatrice. "And we've kept our side of the bargain; you have the Claw. Now you can let us take Torcher home!" She stood up and rattled the portcullis.

Ignatius strode back towards the dragon statue. The Claw was still in the socket. He tried to pull it himself a few times, then lifted it out, weighing it in his hand for a moment.

"But I don't have the *real* Dragon's Claw, do I?" My heart stopped as Ignatius spoke these words. "It doesn't work. Why doesn't the treasure chamber open?" he asked menacingly. Then he let out a deafening bellow that echoed around the hall. "Because this is the replica that my grandfather made!"

Even Torcher stirred at this. Beatrice knelt by him and

shook him gently. "That's right, Torcher. We need you to wake up now." But the chick made no further movement.

Ignatius Crook gave another ugly smile. "How can you be sure that the dragon you are stroking really is Torcher?" he asked, before suddenly snatching out a jewelled wand from beneath the folds of his cloak. He flicked some specks of sparkling dragon dust into the cell, flourished the wand in a figure of eight, and cried, *"Abra!"*

The dragon's eyes opened at once, and we saw straight-away that something was wrong. Torcher's eyes were dark green. This dragon also had eyes of green, but they were a brighter, emerald green, spotted with flecks of gold. Its pupils were like deep black pools, and I could feel myself drawn towards them. I felt drowsy and was beginning to lose my bearings. Then I snapped to. The creature was trying to hyp-notise me! I knew I had to pull my gaze away. "It's the basi-lisk!" I warned. "Whatever you do, don't look it in the eye."

At this, the creature clambered to its feet, hissing and snorting and glaring at me with its startling eyes. Luckily, I had been hypnotised once before and knew exactly what was happening.

"Mr. Tibbs!" Beatrice cried. "Mr. Tibbs, do something!"

Tibbs pointed his pistol in the basilisk's direction and focused to shoot it right between the eyes. But Crook moved quickly. He raised the wand and pointed it at Tibbs, with a cry of *"Ipna!"*

The basilisk immediately turned to focus on Mr. Tibbs.

"Don't look at it; don't let it get you!" I cried.

But it was already too late. Mr. Tibbs's arm fell to his side, and the pistol slipped out of his hand and onto the floor. He took a couple of steps forwards, then staggered to the wall and slumped onto the ground just next to the opening of the portcullis.

"It's hypnotised him," Beatrice wailed. "What are we going to do?"

"We're on our own now, Bea," I said gravely. "We've got to make sure it doesn't get us, too."

The basilisk turned to fix its gaze upon me once more, venom dripping from its fangs. Its hot breath stank. I backed away to the far side of the cell, keeping Beatrice behind me and sheltering her with my body as best I could. The basilisk tugged at the thick chain around its neck, but it held fast.

"*Cambia ziphoni!*" Ignatius ordered, pointing his wand at the basilisk once more.

The basilisk began to change. Its mouth grew longer and thinner. Its leathery wings sprouted feathers.

"It's taking on the form of a cockatrice!" Beatrice exclaimed.

"And it still wants to hypnotise us!" I warned. "But we mustn't let it." I knew how to protect myself, but Beatrice had not been hypnotised before, and I knew she could quickly fall under the basilisk's influence if she gazed at it for more than a moment. "What's four thousand, six hundred and twenty-nine divided by three?" I asked Beatrice.

There was a pause. "One thousand, five hundred and forty-three," she replied.

"Good," I continued. "Now, one million, seven hundred and thirty-three thousand plus two million, eight hundred and forty-two." I knew that the secret to overcoming hypnotism was making continuous, furious calculations in your head. I fired questions at Beatrice and answered them in my own head at the same time.

Thick droplets of venom dripped from the cockatrice's beak. It made a pecking lunge that I managed to dodge whilst still chanting sums and calculating the answers. It reared its head back for another vicious peck.

"Twenty-nine," yelled Beatrice in answer to my most recent question. Then she addressed Ignatius desperately. "Let us out!" she shouted. "We'll do whatever you want."

"Unfortunately, I cannot oblige," said Ignatius. "Since you have failed to bring me what I needed, you are of no use to me now. The poor cockatrice is starving. I think it is time for his supper."

"But we can bring you the real Claw," I tried. "We know where it is."

"Don't be ridiculous, Daniel. I know you would say anything now to save your own skin."

"Dr. Drake is on his way," warned Beatrice. "He won't let you get away with this."

I inched my way around the cell wall towards the portcullis, keeping Beatrice behind me all the while. The cockatrice kept coming towards us until, with a loud *clink,* it reached the end of its chain. It snapped its beak at me and tried desperately to focus its cold eyes on mine. It didn't seem to understand that I could not be hypnotised. Raising its head back once more, it jerked forwards again, yanking violently on the chain, which seemed firmly fixed in place by a bolt in the wall. But then a large crack began to appear in the wall; it spread outwards from the bolt.

"Ugh, I am growing tired of this." Ignatius pretended to yawn. He waved his wand once more. *"Cambia vipera!"*

The chain rattled again as the cockatrice began to change form. Its legs and chest started to bulge with growing muscles, and its feathers melted back into hard scales. Meanwhile its wings opened out like a monstrous umbrella as it grew taller and taller, until the wings were squashed against the roof of the cell. Beatrice and I pressed ourselves up against the wall, and the creature began leering down at us.

"It's turning into a wyvern!" I cried in horror. Normally wyverns had good relationships with humans, but this one would have the mind of a basilisk. It would be huge and deadly.

"Ataca!" ordered Ignatius.

The dragon lunged powerfully forwards, desperately yanking at the chain, which, to our enormous relief, held fast. It roared with frustration.

Somewhere nearby, another dragon gave an answering roar.

"Torcher!" Beatrice and I both exclaimed at once.

The dragon chick must have heard us, for he roared again.

"He can't be far away!" I shouted.

"It makes no difference if we're trapped in here," cried Beatrice. She grabbed the bars, desperately trying to hoist the portcullis open, but it was useless; the iron gate must have weighed close to a ton.

"*Ataca!*" ordered Ignatius once more.

The wyvern gave such an almighty roar that I thought my eardrums might burst. It strained with all its might against the chain that bound it to the wall, until the stone around the bolt started to crumble.

We heard Torcher roar again.

"Mr. Tibbs!" Beatrice peered through the bars as far as she could. "Mr. Tibbs, you have to wake up! The wall is collapsing!"

"Ignatius!" I cried. "Please!"

The wyvern strained forwards in one last terrific effort and pulled the bolt free. The wall that had held it began to buckle, and then a few blocks loosened next to the portcullis. We managed to push them sideways so that they left a small gap in the wall. I struggled to try to help Beatrice through to the other side, but it was no use.

With a thundering crash, an entire section of the back wall tottered and then collapsed. The wyvern bounded towards us with a triumphant roar, only to disappear under a shower of dust and falling masonry.

"Are you all right, Bea?" I cried.

"*I'm* fine," Beatrice answered. "I just need to know what's happening to Torcher."

As if responding to the mention of his name, the dragon chick suddenly poked his head through the hole in the back wall, and he came scampering through. Bravely, he placed himself between the wyvern and the two of us and stood there defiantly, as if challenging it to a fight.

I reached out to try to grab Torcher and pull him away, but I could not hold him. "It's the basilisk, Torcher!" I told him. "You can't fight it. You can't even breathe fire at the moment."

Then I remembered something. My hand darted to my pocket, and I drew out the flint and iron pyrites that I had brought with me. "Here, Torcher, take these, quickly." I held them out to him, and in seconds he had slipped them into his cheek. A moment later, experimental sparks were tickling his lips. He flicked his tail backwards and forwards, then released a sudden powerful jet of flame, causing the wyvern to withdraw for a moment.

But it was soon advancing towards us once more.

"*Terminus ultra,*" cried Ignatius, pointing the wand in our direction. "Finish them!"

"This is the end, isn't it, Bea?" I turned to my sister.

"I can't think of a way out now," Beatrice answered. She grabbed my hand and squeezed it hard. "At least Ignatius won't get his gold," she said bravely.

The wyvern paused. It sniffed the air and put its head on one side as though it was listening to something.

"Terminus ultra!" ordered Ignatius, but there was a note of uncertainty in his voice now, which had not been there before.

The wyvern roared and readied itself to devour us, but a sudden tremendous crash on the other side of the hall distracted it. The main doors burst inwards, and I was more delighted than ever I could have imagined to see Erasmus march boldly through them.

"Confound and blast those unmentionable tunnels and those unspeakable doors!" Erasmus exclaimed to himself with a roar. "My back will never straighten out properly again." Then he spotted us. "Ah, children, there you are. Has Dr. Drake arrived yet? Do you have the dragon chick?" He seemed not to notice that we were trapped in a prison cell with a gigantic dragon readying itself to eat us.

Ignatius backed towards the statue. The wyvern had turned back towards us.

"Subsisto!" cried Igantius, gesturing towards the wyvern with his wand. At his command, the creature froze, and he turned to us. "Answer quickly. What is that?" he demanded, pointing a wizened finger towards the snow-white dragon.

Erasmus stepped a couple of paces nearer to Crook and politely introduced himself. "I am Erasmus, son of

Brythonnia. I am the Dragon's Apprentice. Who are you?" He looked Ignatius up and down with disgust. "You are no Dragonsbane Knight—that is certain!"

"Ha!" scoffed Ignatius. "It does not matter whether or not I am a Dragonsbane Knight. *You* cannot get through that portcullis, and so the basilisk will kill those children. Unless, of course, you have brought me the Dragon's Claw!"

"I have brought the Claw!" Erasmus answered at last. He pulled out the real Dragon's Claw from under his wing and placed it between his own back feet. I was astounded. How on earth had he managed to fetch it? "I thought to offer it as a trophy for single combat between myself and the greatest of the knights here. But I see that there are no knights here." He paused again. "I do not wish to give it to you. And if you or your dragon slay those children, I shall most certainly slay you. I care nothing for the pact between dragons and humans."

"Then perhaps you and I can make a new pact," cried Ignatius, eyeing the Dragon's Claw greedily. "Replace the fake Dragon's Claw that you see on the statue with the real one, and pull it towards you. You may take it away with you afterwards, and I promise to release the children."

"Don't listen to him," cried Beatrice. "He's bluffing."

Erasmus thought for a moment, then said, "I will do as he says. It cannot harm our cause as long as we retain the Claw."

He pulled the replica claw from the statue.

"Now, place the real Claw in the socket," Ignatius instructed anxiously.

Erasmus slotted the Claw into place. It gave a loud *clunk*. Ignatius rubbed his hands together.

"Wait!" Erasmus insisted. "Before I pull the Claw, you will release the children."

Ignatius could see he had little choice. He lowered his wand, then disappeared behind the statue of the dragon and pulled a lever. The portcullis clattered back up into the ceiling. Beatrice and I grabbed Torcher and hurried to Erasmus's side.

"Drop the iron gate again, quickly!" Erasmus insisted.

Ignatius did as he was instructed, and the basilisk was trapped. Beatrice and I looked at each other, then at Torcher, and breathed two huge sighs of relief.

But it was not over yet. Seeing that we were safe, Erasmus pulled the Dragon's Claw towards him. We waited with bated breath. At first nothing seemed to happen, but then came a distant grinding sound, and all at once, a whole section of wall began to slide slowly upwards, so that at first we could just see a thin, glittering line of gold. As it continued to rise, the moving wall revealed a far larger mountain of treasure than I had ever seen in any dragon's lair. Precious metals and gems reached up to the ceiling, and at the very centre of the pile was an ornate silver throne with a carving of a life-size golden *lung* dragon draped around it. In its claws it held a diamond that exceeded even the dimensions of that held by the Dragon's Claw. The jewels were the combined fortunes of all the lost dragons of Britain. My eyes watered at the sight.

Even Ignatius seemed to have difficulty believing he

had really found the hoard at last. "The Lost Treasure of Dragonsbane!" he murmured as he began advancing towards it. "Let me see how the throne suits me!" he cried as he started climbing the golden mountain to reach it. "At last I have come into my inheritance and achieved that which my father failed to do!"

As he lowered himself onto the throne, his breathing became a little irregular and he began to giggle with uncontrollable excitement.

His giggles did not last long, however. The arm of the *lung* dragon carved on the throne suddenly snapped over Ignatius's own arms, and its legs fastened themselves around his legs. "Wh-what's happening?" he murmured helplessly as the chair began to tip over, gradually gaining momentum until it swiftly disappeared from sight. We heard one last strangled shriek, then there was silence and the chair swung back into place — empty.

For a moment, we stood and stared at the space where Ignatius had just been. Then came a slight creak, followed by a low rumble, and a trickle of trinkets tumbled from the vast pile and rattled across the floor. As the rumbling grew louder, more trinkets advanced in our direction. A sudden rush of movement saw the throne disappear in an avalanche of gold. It soon became apparent that the whole treasure pile was slowly sliding towards us.

"The whole place is booby-trapped!" I shouted.

A single stone right at the apex of the domed ceiling fell

with a crushing thud to the ground, narrowly missing Mr. Tibbs. Perhaps the gold had been supporting the roof of the hall all along. The mighty statue of the dragon tottered, then crashed forwards into the middle of the room, knocking over a lectern I had not noticed before. An ancient-looking book tumbled to the ground and was at once buried in falling masonry. The falling statue dragged with it the chain that opened the portcullis. The bars slid up into the ceiling, and the wyvern, which had begun to pace about again, was free to escape. It tiptoed out of its cage and began advancing towards us once more.

"Look out!" I shouted to Beatrice and Torcher. "The whole hall is collapsing!"

"What about the wyvern?" said Beatrice.

"Maybe we could stop it with Crook's wand!" I cried.

Beatrice glanced about the hall wildly. "I think it's disappeared with him; we don't have time to stop and look for it!"

With blocks falling from the ceiling and the statue crashing to the ground, Mr. Tibbs finally seemed to come to. Though he was still in a trancelike state, he managed swiftly to snatch up his pistol and fire a shot at the advancing wyvern. The bullet merely glanced off the wyvern's scales, but it caused the creature to retreat into a corner.

I struggled to help Mr. Tibbs to his feet, whilst Beatrice hurried towards a pair of doors. But they had slammed shut as the hall had begun to crumble, and though she tried with all her might, Beatrice could not budge them. "Erasmus," I cried as I pulled Mr. Tibbs along with me, "the doors!" The young frost dragon threw back his head, then lowered it and charged at the doors, like a bull. They buckled on the second attempt.

By now large blocks of masonry were falling about our heads, and one of the pillars supporting the roof of the hall tottered and fell inwards. Beatrice grabbed hold of Torcher and ran towards the doorway. The wyvern was starting to advance towards us again, and I jerked Tibbs out of the way just in time to avoid a spurt of flame from its mouth.

Rocks were now falling from the ceiling thick and fast. At the far end of the room, the wall had completely collapsed, and an enormous pile of coins was flowing like golden lava, covering the floor of the hall.

"Quick!" Beatrice cried.

I sprinted headlong for the doorway, pushing Mr. Tibbs ahead of me, whilst the wyvern raced after us. Mr. Tibbs made it through a gap between the doors, but just as I was about to follow him, the wyvern leapt into the air, and I felt its claws and its hot breath on my face. There was nothing I could do. I waited for its fangs to sink into my flesh, steeling myself for the horror and the pain. But they did not come. The wyvern was suddenly frozen in midair, and a gentle muzzle was nudging me through the door out of harm's way.

It took me a moment to realise that Erasmus had frozen the wyvern with a blast of his icy breath. I turned to thank him, my heart pounding with relief, but he merely shoved me farther towards our escape tunnel. From the corner of my eye, I saw a rushing tidal wave of gold bury the frozen basilisk.

But we were still not safe. We had escaped to an ante-chamber that led back to the catacomb tunnels, but cracks were already spreading across its ceiling. I grabbed one of the torches from the wall with one hand and guided Mr. Tibbs with the other, wondering how much time we had left.

"I think the entire catacomb is going to collapse!" I told Beatrice.

As if to confirm my suspicions, a huge crash sounded, and the lintel on one of the antechamber doors buckled. Gold coins spilled into the chamber after us.

"Come on!" I shouted.

"Where to?" Beatrice answered helplessly. "We can't go back the way we came, and we don't know another way out."

"Try to stay calm and follow me." Erasmus's voice echoed behind him as he disappeared down one of the tunnels that led from the antechamber.

Beatrice grabbed Mr. Tibbs's free hand, and we hurried after Erasmus, back into the maze of tunnels, with Torcher scampering along behind us and masonry hurtling about our ears.

CHAPTER FOURTEEN

IDRAIGIR'S JUDGEMENT

The notion that any creature other than man can speak
with language, or form societies, or understand history,
or appreciate art, or partake in any of those things that
sets man apart from beast is a notion that must be
quietly but firmly suppressed.

—— *Malleus Draconis (The Hammer of the Dragons), Edvardus Rex*

Working our way out of the Dragon Catacombs was
a terrifying ordeal. With cracks appearing in the
tunnels around us, it was impossible to know which was the
safest route to take. Having to bundle Mr. Tibbs along with
us slowed us down immeasurably. He showed no real sign
of regaining his senses, and as soon as we had pulled him
clear of one barrage of collapsing bricks, it seemed Erasmus
had to lift him over giant cracks that were appearing at our
feet. As one section of tunnel caved in behind us, a rush of air
blew out our torch. We groped in the dark for what felt like
an age before Torcher managed to relight it for us. Luckily,
Erasmus seemed always to know which way to go, and he

led us onwards until we found ourselves in a part of the catacombs that I was sure we had not passed through on our way
into the Grand Lodge.

"How do you know the way?" I asked Erasmus.

"Ah, you see," the frost dragon replied, obviously pleased
with himself, "I have memorised Mr. Anderson's map. Did
you not spot that there was a second entrance marked upon
it? It was the one that Dragonsbane used to bring dragon
captives to their hall to bait and slay."

"To bait and slay?" cried Beatrice. "But that's horrible."

"Indeed, Beatrice, the practises of the Dragonsbane
Knights were frightful. I am in no way sorry to see their hideous cemetery demolished, but for one or two relics I should
have liked to save."

"By relics, do you mean the Dragon's Claw?" I enquired
innocently. Erasmus's reaction astounded me. He stopped
dead in his tracks and turned slowly towards me, a look of
dread and horror on his pure-white face.

"The Dragon's Claw!" he wailed forlornly. "Dr. Drake
entrusted it to my care. He feared the tunnels would be too
narrow for a dragon the size of the great Idraigir. I promised to guard the Claw with my life, but I have"—Erasmus
choked on his words—"left it under the rubble of the
Grand Lodge, never to be seen again." The young dragon
slumped to the ground. For a moment he seemed to lose the
will to carry on, but then he rose purposefully to his feet.
"No, I must try to save it. First I lost Torcher; now the Claw.

If I do not return with both, I am not worthy of the title Dragon's Apprentice."

Erasmus began striding back through the rubble. Torcher scampered after him. We had to stop them. "Erasmus," I pleaded, "we need you. If you go back now, this is the last we will see of you. No human or creature could possibly survive the collapse of the Grand Lodge and all the tunnels around it. Your going back would make things worse for all of us."

Erasmus hung his head. "Then I have failed," he said.

"We have Torcher," I replied firmly. "He was our reason for coming here, and we have achieved our aim."

We continued on our way more slowly than ever, with Erasmus sighing deeply as he exhaled each breath. After just a few more twists and turns, I was surprised to find that we had emerged onto an underground railway track.

"So this is the second entrance," exclaimed Beatrice, relieved at last to have a little daylight to see by.

"Why wasn't it discovered when the railway was built?" I asked, puzzled.

"Because it was buried under a thick pile of rubble," Erasmus explained. "They had no idea what it was hiding. But I knew, of course, and I cleared it away before entering the catacombs to rescue you and Torcher."

A dull rumbling sound came from inside the tunnels; more masonry was falling, and the tunnel now seemed completely blocked. I looked around to check that Torcher was safe, but he was nowhere to be seen.

"Torcher?" I called.

Beatrice heard me and began looking about for him. "Where is he?" she cried, finding it hard to keep control of her voice.

"I thought he was right behind us." I was panicking now. "But it's a while since I looked." I began to understand how Erasmus must have been feeling. I could not believe that I had let Torcher down so badly.

"He could be trapped under some rubble in there," Beatrice said fearfully as she stared back into the black tunnel.

"Then we shall go back and find him," said Erasmus boldly. "Follow me."

"How can we go?" said Beatrice. "There is no way through."

"Then we have failed in everything we set out to achieve," I admitted. "We have lost Torcher. We have lost the Dragon's Claw. Ignatius Crook may be dead, but he has still gotten the better of us."

From deep within the catacombs came a further crashing, rumbling sound as the last tunnel fell in on itself. Stones that had survived centuries were crumbling to dust as they collapsed. Torcher was somewhere beneath that rubble. I felt an uncontrollable sob well up in my chest.

I watched helplessly as a crack started forming in the tunnel we had just left. It started to spread along the ceiling, and I could see the whole tunnel begin to split in two. I fought back tears as I watched the crumbling bricks and mortar. It was hopeless. We would never see Torcher again.

As I stared back along the crumbling tunnel, I saw something moving in the distance. It was coming towards us rather than falling from the ceiling or collapsing inwards from the walls. It seemed human, or animal—or both! My heart pounded with anticipation. As the movement came closer, I was at last sure of what it was, and I called to the others.

"Beatrice, Erasmus, Mr. Tibbs! Torcher has survived! And he's with Dr. Drake! I can see them coming along the tunnel towards us!"

"Hello," cried a familiar cheerful voice as though nothing had happened. "We are here. We are safe! But, goodness me, that was rather too close for comfort."

"Dr. Drake!" exclaimed Beatrice, rushing to fling her arms about him. "What on earth were you doing in there?"

"Well, I wasn't about to leave you lot to face Dragonsbane alone, was I?"

"Torcher!" I cried as the little chick flew out of the tunnel and began running around us all in excited circles. I had to stop Mr. Tibbs from following the dragon chick with his eyes, for fear his hypnotic state would endure even longer.

"I never thought I would be so glad to see a human being." Erasmus smiled as Dr. Drake shook him warmly by the claw. "Or a dragon chick, come to that! However, I think you should know straightaway," Erasmus continued, taking a deep breath before his confession, "that I have failed in the task you entrusted to me."

I was not sure how Dr. Drake would react, but I certainly did not expect him to smile broadly. However, that is exactly what he did. He then thrust his hand inside his jacket and pulled out the Dragon's Claw.

Erasmus was speechless with relief and gratitude. "It's all right, Erasmus," Dr. Drake reassured the young dragon. "I still hold you responsible for Torcher's disappearance, but you have more than made up for it by your courageous actions today. You are a most worthy Dragon's Apprentice, and I shall be sure to tell that to Idraigir and to dragons and dragonologists alike."

A further rumbling sound stopped our merry chatter, but this time it did not come from within the catacombs. "I think we should get out of *this* tunnel quickly," warned Erasmus. "A train is coming!"

Dr. Drake led us out to the safety of a railway embankment. He ordered Erasmus to take Torcher home without delay. "And this time, don't lose him!" he warned. "Daniel, Beatrice and I will take Mr. Tibbs back to Wyvern Way before we return to St. Leonard's Forest." He turned to lead us back into the daylight, chatting as we went.

"I am so relieved that you are both safe," Dr. Drake said with a frown, "but it was foolhardy of you to rush in without me."

"We had to save Torcher," Beatrice explained. "Time was running out, and you hadn't come. Mr. Tibbs wanted to go into the catacombs on his own, but we persuaded him to take us with him."

Dr. Drake looked across at the confused Mr. Tibbs. "And a good job, too, by the look of it." He laughed. "Tibbs is an expert in dragonological theory, but the practical side of things is not really his forte!"

"What about you, Dr. Drake?" I asked. "What kept you?"

Dr. Drake sighed. "Ah, it is all a long story," he began as we turned onto a busy street. "Things became very dangerous and complicated with Mr. Anderson, and so it took us an age to reach Wharncliffe. When we finally arrived at the lair, Erasmus was waiting for us. He is a young, fast-moving dragon, and we felt we should entrust him with the Dragon's Claw in order to speed up Torcher's rescue. Idraigir and I flew after him as quickly as we could."

"And how did you escape the catacombs?" I enquired.

"Well . . ." Dr. Drake looked serious suddenly. "I should still be in there now had it not been for Torcher." By the way he spoke, I could tell the little chick had impressed Dr. Drake. "I met him in one of the tunnels as I was trying to get out. He already had the Dragon's Claw in his mouth. The tunnel ahead was blocked, but he seemed to know the way. I could do little else but follow him."

Dr. Drake hailed a hansom carriage, and we all hopped in. We dropped Mr. Tibbs off at Dragonalia, giving strict instructions to Mr. Flyte to bombard him with complicated calculations until he was back to his old grumbling self again. Then we headed for the railway station.

The journey back to Dragonsbrook flew by, as we had so much to discuss with Dr. Drake.

"I still find it hard to believe that Ignatius Crook was behind Dragonsbane all along," he mused. "And I was so sure we had seen the last of him."

"After everything that happened today," I said wearily, "I am sure we will not be seeing Ignatius again."

"It is a sad end to an unhappy life," observed Dr. Drake. I was impressed that, despite everything Ignatius Crook had tried to do to him, Dr. Drake was still able to sympathise with his enemy.

It was early evening by the time Beatrice and I returned to Dragonsbrook. As we pushed open the rusty gate and entered the garden, a red, scaly bundle flew at us, almost knocking Beatrice off her feet.

"It's good to see you, too, Torcher!" she said. "Anyone would think we'd been apart for months!"

The cottage looked cosy and welcoming, with smoke billowing from the chimney and gaslights shining in the parlour window. I pushed open the door and hurried into the kitchen, where our parents were waiting for us. We were overjoyed to see them; we had so much to tell them!

"Mother! Father!" I cried.

"We met the queen!" said Beatrice.

"And we thought Mr. Tibbs was a traitor. . . ." I added.

"But he wasn't; it was Ignatius Crook. . . ." Beatrice continued.

Father held up a hand to stop our animated chatter. "Erasmus has told us everything," he said sternly. "You had no business following Tibbs into the catacombs like that."

I hadn't expected a telling off, but I supposed it was no more than we deserved. I looked at Mother. She was trying hard to seem cross, but I could tell she was really pleased and relieved to see us.

"Oh, come here, you two," she said, laughing, and she swept us into her arms. "We're so glad you're safe."

"And we're very proud of you," Father added with a smile. "Though I'm not sure we will ever dare leave you on your own again."

The following day, an invitation came for us all to visit Dr. Drake that afternoon. After lunch, we set off with Torcher for Castle Drake. There was a large gathering of people on Dr. Drake's lawn. Lord Chiddingfold was there, as was the Prime Minister. I recognised many of the others from the S.A.S.D. dinner.

Being the only dragon there, Torcher hid himself under a table and sulked. We would have coaxed him out, but Billy and Alicia rushed across to say hello, and we quickly tried to fill them in on everything that had happened since we had last seen them, early the previous day. However, Billy and Alicia had news to tell us.

"It's Mr. Tibbs," said Alicia. "They've had to send him on to the London Mathematical Society. Apparently the basilisk's powers of hypnosis were stronger than we thought. Mr. Flyte kept giving him harder and harder calculations to do, but it didn't make any difference! We've no idea how long he'll have to stay at the society." She giggled.

"It serves him right," I scoffed, "after the way he treated us the other day."

Beatrice had softened towards Tibbs. "But we'd never have found Torcher without him," she reminded me. "And he was right, after all, wasn't he?"

"What do you mean?" I was puzzled.

"Well, he never believed Dragonsbane had re-formed; he always suspected the story was some sort of distraction," Beatrice argued.

I had to admit she was right. Tibbs's theory had been a good one. But on future expeditions, I hoped he would stay in the society's headquarters, where he belonged.

Darcy spotted me, winked, and sauntered over to give me a friendly pat on the back. "What's this all about?" I asked him, nodding towards the gathered throng.

Darcy smiled and simply said, "Wait and see."

Dr. Drake was nowhere to be seen, but I assumed that once he arrived, there would be some sort of announcement.

Suddenly a gasp went up from the crowd. I looked up to see Idraigir coming in to land on the lawn, accompanied on one side by Erasmus and on the other by Brythonnia.

"It must be an important occasion for Brythonnia to come all this way," Billy observed.

As soon as Idraigir landed, Torcher poked his head out from under the table and ran up to greet him. The two dragons rubbed noses.

At last I saw Dr. Drake emerge from the house and stride across the lawn to stand next to Idraigir. The Guardian Dragon straightened himself up and looked expectantly towards his audience. Excited chatter quietened to an expectant hush as the great dragon prepared himself to speak.

"*Praisich hoyari,*" Idraigir announced gravely. "Would Daniel and Beatrice Cook please step forwards?"

Beatrice and I looked at each other apprehensively before following Idraigir's instruction.

The Guardian Dragon had a stern expression on his face. "You have been disobedient," he boomed. "As has my young apprentice here." Erasmus bowed his head, and my heart sank. This was not to be a celebration after all; instead we were to be humiliated in front of the whole of the S.A.S.D. "You are guilty of risking your lives to save a dragon you loved, when you had been told not to. Erasmus committed an even greater crime, for by his actions, he allowed that dragon chick to fall into the hands of our enemies. Lord Chiddingfold has asked me to administer justice to all three of you."

"Justice?" I whispered. I dreaded his next words.

"Justice," the Guardian continued, "such as it is. For, by your actions, the dragon chick was rescued and Ignatius Crook's wicked plot was thwarted once and for all. You have shown great courage in the face of extreme adversity. Yet none of us may rest easily, for the danger to dragons grows daily. Alexandra Gorynytchka still presents a grave threat. To counter that threat, we need the strongest forces we can command. Are the three of you ready to help us?" Idraigir demanded.

"Of course we are," we answered without question.

"Then this is the judgement: you will travel to the North for your own safety. Your parents will accompany you. Erasmus will become your tutor for a time. He still has much to learn about humans and their ways. And so, in a way, you two will also become *his* tutors."

I looked at Erasmus. At first he seemed to be happy at the prospect, but when he saw me looking, he scowled. I knew he was bluffing. Over the past two days he had grown fond of us, and we of him. Not so long ago I would have thought our punishment unbearable, but now I welcomed it, especially as we should be serving the S.A.S.D.

"But first," said Dr. Drake, "we have a message from Her Majesty Queen Victoria. Yesterday, Her Majesty informed our Prime Minister that she wished to bestow an honour upon Beatrice and Daniel Cook." He turned to speak to us directly. "As a result, I am pleased to announced that from this day forward, the two of you are to be considered Drago-nologists, First Class."

For once, both Beatrice and I were speechless. What could we say? One moment, we were being punished; the next, we were being awarded one of the highest honours a dragonologist can hope to achieve.

"Now," concluded Dr. Drake, "before your investiture, there is one other small matter to which I must attend. I have a letter for you, and I would like you to read it so that everyone here can hear its contents."

He handed us a sheet of paper. At the top was a coat of arms featuring a lion and a unicorn. Beatrice and I glanced at each other, our faces aglow. It was from the queen herself. We each took hold of one side of the paper, and together we read,

"To Daniel and Beatrice Cook—
By Royal Command

It has come to our attention that the two of you, through your brave actions, have been of very great service to our realm, to its subjects, and to the dragons living within it. We there-fore congratulate you on your well-deserved promotion to the rank of Dragonologists, First Class. We are sure that you will fulfil the role and carry out your duties admirably and con-tinue to be a credit to our nation. I will always remember with fondness the day two children arrived by dragon in Buckingham Palace Gardens, and I very much look forward to seeing you again one day and hearing more of your dragonological adventures.

In the meantime, I wish you the very best of luck. May you be ever successful in your dealings with dragons, may you conserve and protect them wherever they may be found, and may you keep safe, secret, and silent at all times.

In the Name of the Secret and Ancient Society of Dragonologists, Go with Dragon Speed,
Her Royal Highness,
Queen Victoria."

It had been a most remarkable few days, full of drama and excitement. Despite the danger and some of the sights we had seen, we would not have swapped the experience for the world. Now, with Idraigir's judgement, we knew that our dragonological adventures were far from over. In fact, it seemed they had only just begun.

Don't miss the first two volumes in the fire-breathing

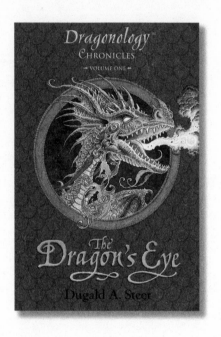

"Dragon lovers will be well pleased." —— *Booklist*

"A companion to *Dragonology* . . . satisfying and charming."
—— *Publishers Weekly*

adventure series, The Dragonology Chronicles!

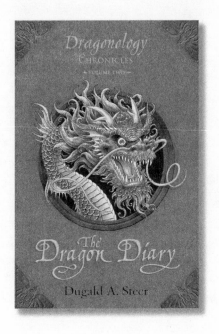

"A fantastic saga for dragon lovers of all ages."
—— *Midwest Book Review*

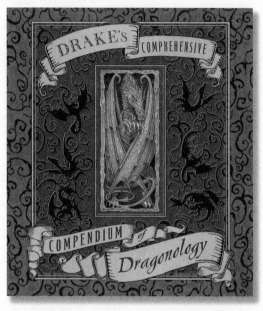

And look for the book that started it all!

For true believers only, here is the original
volume that introduced the world to
Dr. Ernest Drake and his science of dragonology.

Get the complete 'Ology library
Nearly 16.5 million books in print